GODLIKE

© 2005 by Richard Meyers

Thanks for their help to Sheelagh Bevan, Noel Black, and Michael DeCapite.

Grateful acknowledgement is made for permission to use the following:

p. 31, "Yesterday I Saw a Man" from *Rene Ricard 1979–1980*. © 1979 by Rene Ricard.
Reprinted by permission of the author.

p. 52, "The Silence at Night" from *Collected Poems* by Edwin Denby. © 1975
by Edwin Denby. Reprinted by permission of the estate of Edwin Denby.

p. 46, "Detach, Invading," p. 68, an excerpt from "Tone Arm," and p. 68, "More of
This Light," from *New & Selected Poems, 1963–1992* by Ron Padgett. © 1995 by Ron
Padgett. Reprinted by permission of David R. Godine, Inc.

p. 132, excerpt from "A Name Day" from *Collected Poems* by James Schuyler.
© 1993 by the estate of James Schuyler. Reprinted by permission of
Farrar, Straus and Giroux, LLC.

Thanks for their generosity to Yvonne Jacquette and Christopher Wool.

Published by Akashic Books
ISBN-13: 978-1-888451-77-1; ISBN-10: 1-888451-77-7
Library of Congress Control Number: 2004115736; All rights reserved
Printed in Canada on acid-free paper; First Printing

Akashic Books
PO Box 1456, New York, NY 10009
Akashic7@aol.com, www.akashicbooks.com

Portions of this book have been published in the magazines *Purple*,
The World, *Bald Ego*, *Vanitas*, *Ecstatic Peace*; the literary ezine *can we have our ball
back?* (www.canwehaveourballback.com); the broadsheet periodical *Accurate Key*
(singlepress); the pamphlet *Weather* (CUZ Editions); the anthologies
Carved in Rock (Thunder's Mouth Press) and *Rimbaud après Rimbaud* (Éditions
Textual); and as the pamphlet *2-D Beckoning* (Angry Dog Midget Editions).

GODLIKE
Richard Hell

GODLIKE

The Hospital Notebooks of Paul Vaughn

incorporating his memoir-novelette of R.T. Wode

I want to make what I know of R.T. and that time into a book so that it won't be gone. I don't have the best memory in the world but there is no reason I can't produce a story as close to true as it would be if these things happened yesterday. It will just have mixed into it what I have become across twenty-five years, but that includes what I've learned, and at least I can say with certainty that it's written with love and without any hidden purposes or self-censorship.

Those are more or less the first words in the first of the notebooks I filled during the month I was in the hospital in 1997. I planned to write about T. in the form of a novel. I wrote other things in the notebooks besides my story of T., too: letters, diaries, poems, even an essay. Now I've accepted my editor's encouragement and made this book out of all of it.

As an account of T., it will have to do, because T. is gone and only he could offer a memory to compare. I've known for a long time the meaning of the deaths of friends. It's losing oneself! T. took me with him, but I've been what I can, and I want to present my him before it's too late for me too.

Look, he was a scumbag. Nearly everybody hated him. He didn't care! He insisted on it. That's the beauty of it. But it's important that you not like him either. If you like him, you don't understand him. To give offense was his mission, his meaning. That was part of his failure, the impossibility of him; I don't advocate it—it's just what he was. I do maintain that it's interesting. But then, a good writer can make anything interesting.

It makes me think of movie stars. People say James Dean was the same way, mean and arrogant and competitive. And I remember having this revelation watching Bette Davis on-screen one time. That everything that was magnificent about her in the movie would be impossibly obnoxious in the same room with you ...

Paul Vaughn
NYC, 2004

1

It was March and the weather was like a pornographic high-fashion magazine. But Raw's Drink was a gutter derelict in it. The room was see-through brown broken by a debris of battered tables and cluttered walls. There was a little clearing in the far corner where a stalk of microphone stood leaning thinly.

Paul felt affection for the poor poets, his family. He probably liked them more than anyone else did. He was popular for that.

Tonight's reader was Tom Bennett. Tom was a filthy drug addict who was too smart for his own good. His face was like a monkey's carved from a blond wood doorstop wedge, he was going bald, and he wore reddish whiskers that looked like pond scum. He never stopped talking and he considered himself a Buddhist. Whatever else, he was in his element at Raw's this night, and it was heartening. He was a messenger and Paul was mentally gorging on it. "God made everything from nothing, but the nothing shows through."

Paul played a favorite mental trick for enjoying poetry readings and imagined the reader had died long ago.

The reading ended, and everyone drank on, and the room got

noisier. People went out into the air and smoked grass together and came back. Paul saw the kid. He planned to find him but hadn't gotten around to it when he sensed the attention shifting in the crowd. The kid'd gone up to three different poets in the room and told each what he thought of him. He told Bill Miller, "I read your latest book and all I can say is that your only virtue is its own punishment." He told Barret Combs that he'd "ruined frivolity for a generation." Then he gave each of the poets hand-copied examples of a new poem and told them that they could suck his cock for $20. He arrived at Paul, and just as Paul realized who he was the kid introduced himself. He was the boy who'd sent him a letter a few weeks before. The letter had read:

Mr. Vaughn! Sir!

I write to you most humbly, most presumptuously. I am no one except that I am a poet. And it is because I am a poet that I eat up your books. And that is why I write and enclose the pages you find here. I hope that you will respond to them.

I'm going nuts in this nowhere. Used to be I could twist in my misery and big time lusts, sweating, and the breezes of these suburban streets would cool me a little, the fruity sunsets would bring me something, as would old literature, but now I know too much! One must always move on. (It is not important to live.) I'm rotting here! I will come to New York. Especially since I know of you.

Do you know what I mean that I am no one except

that I am a poet? I will explain so that you cannot mis-
understand. I do not want to be anyone. I have nothing to protect. I want to see and be seen through. I am
given to see and I see aloud. It is necessary that "I," that
cowardly imposition, be discarded, in order that
nothing interfere, that nothing interrupt, that nothing pollute what speaks. It isn't pretty! But it is poetry
and all we know of– of–. I know you know what I
mean.

Have mercy on me.

Your admiring little bro,

Randall Terence Wode

Paul had written back and told the kid he should come to New
York and to call him when he got there.
   "I am drunk," the boy said.
   "You are?"
   He lowered his voice. "Come outside and walk with me."
   They left the party behind and the air outside was a nice surprise. The presents kept coming, piling up around them as they
walked. Paul got breathless and aroused.
   R.T. told him his big ideas. He said honestly there were only two
or three poets and that he himself was first among the living, with
the possible exception of Paul, though he was in danger of going
slack. He talked of how the literary was sacred but the literary was
shit. That the poets' poor knowledge must be *advanced in life* for
poetry to be real. That the poem is everything, but incidental–it's

shit and come, it's tracks and mirrors, hair, snot, ricocheting beams. It's nothing, but it's all we get and if we will be receptive it's the thing itself, the nothing itself, and what else is there to desire, want, have, be, and it only follows from delirium, which is just ordinary life. "No big deal," he said, and it was true–Paul'd heard it before (though he hadn't seen it)–"You want to kiss me, don't you." He took Paul's hand and pulled it to him and pressed the palm on his crotch.

They'd stopped and T. was shuffling Paul back toward a dark building wall on East 3rd Street. Paul's heartbeat was out of control. He was taller than T. and he grabbed T.'s ruffled head and bumped his mouth on his. The oddness of male on male was sexy. They almost fell over but the wall got there just in time. The mouth was a scooped-out thing that felt unreal; Paul couldn't adjust, he was still too apart from him, but wanted to feel T.'s cock through his pants and when he did that it went really real for a moment before they separated again.

Paul just wanted to run his finger along the crack of T.'s ass, and T. let Paul turn him to the wall and do that. He reached under and T.'s cock had gotten harder and he squeezed its base through T.'s pants. T. gave Paul charge of himself there for a moment, and Paul took advantage of it by pulling T.'s shoulder to turn him, kissing him once again, and it felt closer to a kiss. Paul started them walking back along the street. He wasn't going to hurry or let T. think he was at his mercy. It was better to stretch it out anyway.

"So how does it feel to be a faggot?" T. asked.

"What? ... Uh ... So far, so good."

"But you always have been."

"Whatever you say ..."

They stumbled into Paul's rooms on Bank Street at about 4:00 A.M.

In the house everything was stagnant and half-size, defensively smug. When the pregnant wife came in, Randall threw up. She screamed and stuttered. She looked inappropriate, like a mangy zoo creature in a fake habitat.

"What a stink," T. said. "That stuff smells ... Let's try to go to sleep." He looked at Paul and suggested, "Why don't you slap that thing."

Paul lurched toward his wife and she fled. Paul turned and grinned as if he'd just scored a goal, started back to T. and slipped in the vomit, then fell to his hands and knees. He laughed. "Ugh." It wasn't too bad. T. sat down in an armchair as Paul got up and put one foot in front of the other toward the kitchen around the corner. When Paul came back with a large wet terrycloth, T. had his penis out and was idly playing with it. As Paul kneeled over the pool of vomit he looked at the penis and then at T.'s face. He put his hand down his own pants, but no, he wanted to wipe up the mess. The smell stung, but for a second he liked it: scent of death rot, home, was the sticky inside of his own asshole when he stuck a finger in it masturbating. He was getting a kind of hardon, but he threw the towel over the vomit and tried to wrap it up. His wife scurried through the room holding a soft little overstuffed bag. When she saw them she recovered her dignity for a moment in amazement, and for that moment Paul sank and groaned inside but T. was tougher, and she retired from the house with a sad squeal.

Paul crawled over and pulled T.'s cock in between his lips. He filled his mouth with it most gratefully and T. gazed at him with contempt that was tremendous and delicious. Paul was still a little bit ashamed and that's what made the cruelty right and the perfection of it pooled them together. After all, T. was Paul's admirer, and T. was the grateful one, for being allowed to be mean with love.

The world was young.

And in the morning the sun found them out on the floor of the little parlor entangled and gritty, the faint death-smell of the half-digested food and alcohol mixing with the brute light; bodies God's idle graffito.

2

When they awoke they started drinking again right away. It was a hot day. T. put on an Albert Ayler record and started pulling books off the shelves. He took a Bill Knott, a Borges, a Frank O'Hara, David Shapiro's skinny little *January*, and Ron Padgett's *Great Balls of Fire*, and put them in his knapsack. A couple of times he oddly kissed Paul like a father. Paul cried once.

T. said, "Today the theme will be time, work, and sex among men. Sex among men is like using your wood to make a violin."

They walked up Seventh Avenue toward Paul's bank on Sheridan Square like corporeal beings among the ghosts, or melodic rustling in the silence. It was cloudy, the sky a bruised white that shone too hard to look at. Below it, buildings and streets were pounded from dead hard matter that felt like paining smacks, with all those quaint and obnoxious announcements posted on them in such determined effort to infiltrate and influence people. It occurred to Paul that T. was speaking to him that way: proclaiming himself and trying to enter and take his mind. But he knew he'd been raised a level, and the puke-flecked boy was all the sweeter-seeming for having his behavior seen through unbeknownst.

Paul withdrew a little money at the bank and then nudged T. through the angular small streets in the direction of Washington Square.

"Look," said T., "What do you think of that?" There before them was a garbage can with a glossy damaged issue of the *New Yorker* topping the pile of trash. It was open to a picture of a sparkling braceletted wrist and an impossibly elegant woman's face. The scripture read, "Diamonds Are Forever."

"This is the hotel I was thinking of."

In the tiny room they lay in the narrow bed. It had started raining outside and the smell of it came in puffs under the doubly dirty raised window.

Paul said, "Your program sounds like a lot of work. The good life is lazy," his arm under T.'s head. T. had his elbow bone in Paul's ribs.

"Pure receptivity has a highly valued place in my system."

"Uh."

"I think we're through, Vaughn. You're uptight or something or we're in different places and it's hopeless. Maybe we should get someone else in here to perk up our relationship."

"Like that desk clerk?"

"Yeah, I bet he knows where the drugs are too. I'd suck him off … So what's this big idea?"

"It's kind of the opposite of yours … or the other side of the coin …"

"What we need is a coin with one side."

"You're a coin with one side."

"And all of us are merely players."

"That's stupid. You're ridiculous."

"I beat you to the punch. Aw, I'm sorry. Go ahead and tell me."

"Nothing."

"Don't sulk now—"

Just then there was a knock at the door. Paul and T. looked at each other, their noses too close.

"Who's that?" called T.

Through the door, "It's Larry, the desk clerk."

Paul's eyes had started to water as he looked back at T. T. asked, "Should I open the door naked?" For a second Paul felt like he was losing his mind.

"I don't know."

"I think I should."

"Do it then."

And he did and before long they were all having sex.

So Paul woke up with T. again. The sunlight this second morning was grey again, undone, through the narrow airshaft. Paul had work he had to handle, and a wife with a baby due. There was a half-smoked joint right in arm's reach and a bottle of wine. He saw a tuft of T.'s armpit hair. He had to decide whether to drink or think.

He drank, but he got up to leave anyway. He wrote to T. "Here's $10. I have to go check on things. Thanks. Soon, Later, Love, Paul."

On the way out the door he saw a scrap of paper on the floor. It could be deciphered:

> see the light look into the hole
> cheap hotel room wall to the
> next room past
> the hole in the crack
>
> of the desk clerk's bent rear
> end he's shown us
> the hole damn catalog
> cheap hole tea-room

21

hair-lined butt like a private
eye out in the saliva
to see the light
look into the hole

and then you eat it
I know the taste of light
Red: cock head, Blue: asshole
(clean), Green: eyeball, White: blood

all sweet, all key fund as glances
in an icy tub and I swill it, drenched
in the gushing seen m, the big pissing
over broken head suppository of it

the wack, the tang, the brassiere
the poop eye candle-flame
slick and cold banana popsicle fuck
in the face the eye the prick slit of it

come next May flowered China haunches
flush to fan rhapsodic array
toe carrot pressed further doe
person of a cartoon persuasion bursting too of it

flowers

What?! He cracked a syllable of laugh out loud. T. must've written it the night before. What a night. The writing brought it back.
And it blew him away, poem of his sixteen-year-old boyfriend.

He thought of the sight of T.'s penis, and how it was shocking, like the exhibition of a person's internal things, but so great.

Everything was changed now, though inevitable (as things will be once they've happened). Maybe he shouldn't leave. But he wanted to be out in the morning, and not altogether dependent on T., and he had to do something about his wife and job.

He went, descending the smelly back staircase the flight down. A different desk clerk was on duty. Outside the day was brilliant by Washington Square Park. He felt himself turning in the cold fiery cranks and mechanisms of the new day, like something from a Blake poem or Dante. "Scent of garbage and patchoullie and carbon monoxide…"

**

They call me the Chinese Monkey. Smear me like icing. "Oh fuck, what do I do now?"

Um…

Take a breath now…

I'm a little confused about those days.

My memory's not the best, and I don't trust memory anyway. Randall's dead and my wife hasn't spoken to me in years.

Pink and blue smear. How do people do that (believe in their memories–it's like believing in art)? I remember the feelings, I think. But I'm not who I was twenty-six years ago–I have to imagine that person.

Nothing wrong with that. One's "personality" is continuously being modeled by the, the things that happen. Isn't that right? (It's not like we're instruments that are played, we're like dogs that are trained. Or hairdos. ((I, hairdo.))) Plus one tends to get more selfish and conservative, if maybe less judgmental, upon coming with age to realize one will actually be dying. And I guess I do have an advantage across all these years for having the same genes and experience as the second lead in the story . . .

Then again, maybe there's destiny ("Character is fate"). ("Tomorrow is another day. But then, so was yesterday.") Maybe I'm just too fastidious (yeah, right)—but be that as it may, I wouldn't presume to call it "nonfiction." It's all true though! If the truth be told, I'd rather think about Liv Tyler right now. She's such a distraction. I wonder is her glow subliminally tinged by her name's hint of "Liz Taylor"? Nah—that's pretty far-fetched. Her coltishness—velvety—, and (star-)crossed eyes, her overbite, so lovely it makes my room change color ("teeth to hurt"). That's what we want from a star. How will she age I can't help but wonder. Imagine her with a dick! Wow! (Anyway I've never been so impressed by Liz Taylor. She's for real faggots. I'm not really a faggot. I just have a queer streak. A little fond affection for cock.)

I still do things that I absorbed from Him. Where are the dead? Piled up in me like a logjam? Is that why my chest is dry and hurts, why it's hard to talk? Don't be overdramatic. It's true they (the dead) can take care of themselves, whereas we need to take care of ourselves (each other). Maudlin (word derived from "Mary Magdelene!"). "One's soul is in other people."

Yes, I'm over fifty now!

       and mentally skipping
       around the hospital room
       surprised to be alive
       (don't ask)
       but here-and-now so pleased

to be that suddenly I break
break I tell you, break
into
song like Anna Karina!

Good grief. Sorry. This anesthetic or pain killer (same thing, isn't it?: no-pain=numb) (on top of everything else, I had to have a hernia operation) they have me on is nice, but it has me lulled (and riddled, shuddering, with parentheses)—woozy, giddy, and well-ventilated. I am fond of freesias. I close my eyes and go to the most marvelous places. Opiation. Opiation freesia places. And the universally concupiscent M. Jean-Luc! He's the poster boy for getting old (and making things more and more beautiful and wild, not to say funny, less to say sad ((I don't want to say "deep" at all, as you might imagine))). The window and the freesias are where the eye goes (when not inwards). Freesias Where the Eye Goes. Freesias: those Picabian mechanoerotic clusters like the unlikely so-fragrant flesh-pockets of the air itself (revealed by some colorful method of scientific staining). God, what am I talking about? It is a flower like an old-time movie star (Claudette Colbert, Norma Shearer) with those stunning and elaborate, bright butter-yellow, deceptively delicate heads on those swaying bent thin stalks. But aren't they all? The "stars" altogether more like flowers than stars . . . As penises are . . .

It's funny, I liked the least the other week that picture of Schiele's in the show at the Modern that depicted bare winter branches, like insect-legs' -legs with -legs, in a crackling dry web or network across the canvas, sky—it looked to me like a motel room abstraction—but somehow now it has me finding a similar freezing view from this window so pleasing, which I would have hated before. Viva art.

About writing as acting—but how you can't err (*Individuum est ineffabile*)—how we wondered and worried and gossiped re R. Terence.

See you later (or earlier I mean).

Paul found himself wandering in the direction of his old friend Ted's apartment and so he called him up. Ted asked him to pick up some Lucky Strikes and come on over.

Ted, large in a smudged white t-shirt and unshaven, was squeezing the blankets up to his neck as he lay in the bed that took up most of the apartment's only real room. As Paul entered, the wooden bed was in the far right corner, with narrow pathways beside it against the left wall and at its foot. Next to Paul at the foot of the bed was a typewriter on a tiny table with its kitchen chair, and alongside it a few small overstuffed bookcases covered with papers and ashtrays. A smoking filterless butt hung and bobbed in the corner of Ted's mouth, forcing him to squint his eyes.

"Hi buddy, I just made a new poem and it got me thinking. I want to try a kind of mental suggestion on you, OK? Now I know I'm not a pretty picture, though I have my partisans—but imagine you'd just come from looking at a totally great painting, one that did things in a way you'd never seen in a picture before, that isolated this class of look you'd never noticed, or at least appreciated the greatness of, till now, and to which I, here, am closely enough related in my magnitude and general vista as to thereby reveal to you my own heretofore overlooked and unfairly neglected beauty..."

"Not necessary, Ted."

"Great. You knew all along. I'm glad you see it my way. And you, you too are beautiful..."

"May I ask what's the pill situation?"

"Atrocious."

"Oh."

"And that's the least of it."

"I'm glad you admit that."

"I admit it, son…"

Paul's eyes focused on a piece of notebook paper that was taped to the wall. Scrawled in a big baby-handed script onto it were the words "don't understand" and Paul felt a little dizzy. He felt as if a larger reality was just beyond his comprehension, though possibly reachable. It was trippy. A ringing sound swelled from one ear through his skull to the other. He shuddered, his whole body's position-sense vibrated, and he was momentarily deeply, nicely smeared. He staggered slightly. Ted laughed and asked if he was all right.

"I had a crazy night last night—wait—days, actually, well … two nights and a day …"

"Tell Ted."

He hadn't realized how worn out he was and grateful for a little kindness. He sat down in the wooden kitchen chair he pulled around into the doorway. "I've been with this boy and he has me completely turned around …"

"A boy, huh …"

"It sure is going to make a mess of things."

"What do you mean he has you 'turned around,' exactly? Your butt in his face?"

"Ha ha."

"Well, he makes you dizzy?"

"… Yeah," said Paul nasally.

"Yeah, but you are fucking—or whatever you homosexuals call it—him … ?"

"Well, what am I talking about?"

"That's exciting, or suspenseful anyway. He's the kid at the reading, at the party, right?"

"You know about him?"

"Yeah. I was there, I got there late. People were talking about him. I actually saw you leave with him ... I wondered how long it would take once you got married."

"I know, god damn it. What the hell does it mean? Shit. He already has me half pulled into his psycho way of looking at things. I need a little perspective. On the other hand—"

"What I've got is yours, pal."

"Do you have a drink?"

"A drink? Nope. Sorry."

"What the hell do you have?"

"Me. It. And ... But no butt!"

"Uh ... Ah ... It's all so weird ... Why don't we go to a bar right now. Do you want to go sit at a bar? Like the Blarney Stone on 14th Street?"

"Sure!"

So they went out. Ted had brought his new poem to show Paul. Paul glanced at it, tipsy and preoccupied.

> Most of all I meant to come to you;
> while I was trying my boat got held
> up by a character. I know
> it seems like it's always that way.
> In breezes, at dawn, with the heavy
> metals of the current blasting, I can't
> get a single moving profile right
> or I am tacking and the wheel's awry,
> birds already long awake. For
> you I salvaged the prow and partly wasted

28

coffers of grease. The headings that
expose me to the vagaries of urine
are my own "I am aware."
I yielded to the promises of ha; and
if I run aground it's probably decided
by announcements muses harmonize,
those who have kept me from coming to you.

3

Gee I almost want to start making up a book about Ted. Well, he's in this one.

He's dead too of course. It's so unlikely that I'm alive.

The dead take you with them though. If I don't write about us, it will disappear into nothing forever. (When you think about it, in a way there is no "past" except nothing: complete empty darkness: it's what's actually forgotten, unrecorded, unknown to anyone. The rest of the past is really the present.) Half of it is already gone with those who died (one's "better half").

What a line is "it's so unlikely I'm alive"—everything's unlikely until it happens, and then it's inevitable!—but that's why we like it, I guess, and have now written it twice. It's some kind of odd luck (and luck that will come to an end soon enough).

> The whole city seemed to
> optically snap with the
> cool bright
> ness of the just moist
> light and air ricocheting
> in pings and flapping planes

widely below the sky, in
to which, later, like chairs
broken over heads, giant
graphically depicted
pins and needles, with
splintered breaks like
kindling, the
pretty light and air
rise lightly back up, leaving
nothing but this inhaling chill.

Jeez, that's a sad poem—I wrote it just before I flipped out—but not, because it kind of works.

At dusk the light returns to the sky as your vision will rise up the skirt of a girl as far as possible.

In a way, "art" is just "making the best of things."

Time: the entertainment. "Compelling!" "Irresistible!" "Fascinating!" "Suspenseful!" It is fascinating: that from there one has gotten to this. No, give me pussy and . . . "Yesterday I saw a man / In front of a hotel / Calling, 'Dick, Dick.' / How many times have I / Wanted to stand / On a street corner / And yell for dick?"

These young poets and even some journalists come around to see me or try to. People always think I'm going to die even though I'm really here because of a nervous breakdown. But it's true: I'm not on that Antabuse for nothing, and I had that operation, and I am feeling my age. The visitors I welcome, of course, are the ones who bring me things, gossip included. It'll get them through the door anyway. Sex'll get them furthest. And they want gossip from me too, gossip of the old days. It's almost like I'm the last surviving member of a big-time rock group. My generation is pretty famous, at least here in 1997. The visitors often want stories of Him, though the best are least likely to ask (except the very best, who don't give a damn what they say). As I'm writing the book I tend to bring him up anyway. After all, I wonder too.

I still don't quite understand how well-known he is. How do you gauge that? He's in all those anthologies and all the poets refer to him. He was even a major part of a TV show. At the same time I can only think of him as my friend who was sixteen –the public presence is on another, irrelevant plane like say the way he exists to the IRS or the Social Security system or something ...

I lived and he didn't. There's no virtue in surviving, as war veterans know (and it messes them up).

Tim brought me this book of Godard interviews. Gee, J.-L. makes it feel worthwhile. (I know it is anyway.)

Yesterday I had this moment's wave of fear of dying. I'd forgotten that could happen until it did, and I realized it'd happened before. Think of what happened to Andy Warhol in the hospital! I always think of myself as pretty OK with death—but ... it is infuriating, disrespectful, humiliating! Lonely. My God, everything swept away, blown away, no meaning or purpose, no friend or companion—zip: taken. And no appeal heard. One time all my books got stolen and *that* was traumatic.

Then again maybe one could just be completely brave and casual about it. Obviously that'd be the smart thing. Dying's milk that got spilt a lot of generations ago. But then we are "wired" to consider it the enemy, right?

And the night sky falls into your heart. Which is some kind of ice cream. The heart in flames of dark ice cream. Licked by death. Is this Satan talking?

Why do I try to preserve? There's that theory too, isn't there? I'm making my contribution to the meme-complex, the culture. Maybe I'm singing like a bird. ("I lift my voice in song") ("And I'm just like that bird, singing just for you") I remember crooning to T. (and many others). Drunk, too.

I was a sheet of gold that he hammered.

The answer to a toe that asks the lilac sky-flow ties

The magic of intensest poetry-snot penetrating literature

The numbered-times-in-a-lifetime sudden too-late knowledge that you can be seen by the unseen from the dark because you're in the light

***

My memories seem to migrate to a dead-quiet fall afternoon. I don't know why that is. It's like a single lovely changeless afternoon that is their setting. There's a slight chill and the sky is cloudless.

4

The '60s were springtime in the world, New York, but by 1971 the dog days had arrived. Randall Terence seemed to be pissed off for having left his childhood somewhere (as much as he wanted free of it) and he didn't buy the "love and peace" shit. It all looked like lies, stupidity, and politics to him. He didn't know how young he still was, bitter but naïve. He was so shocked at politics. That's a youth giveaway, that kind of indignation at quid pro quo (and that even the poets practiced it!).

It was clear fast that he wasn't going to succeed with the literary crowd. The poets had made their poet-culture and it was their province to govern even if they were poets. T. thought they were lame and corny and betrayers of the knowledge and he treated them that way. Ted and I were his only real writer friends.

I remember him talking about it, high on pills. "What, what is it? What is it and what am I doing to myself? Can this be what's supposed to happen? That I annoy and piss off everyone and suffer? Yeah."

The world was his fucking pasture. Other people fantasized, other people "perceived," but he *did*. Like Jesus Christ. (There is evil in action—in *doing things*—though, which Christ knew and it was His true guilt.)

Maybe his behavior was ugly, but nothing really young is really ugly.

His ragged company—what little company he kept—turned out to be the lowlifes and street kids, petty thieves and drug-users, musicians and Times Square go-go dancers, as well as the crew of three or four people he liked to see who were full-blown mentally ill and on strong psychopharmaceuticals. T. considered these separated out and parallel people to be the citizens of the interesting world. He was like an obscure and half-assed, filthy Andy Warhol, not of the starstruck but of the truly rejected.

One of his favorite companions was John Schwartz. John was a cheerful, intense young man (was he twenty-three or thirty-five?) of starry delusion. He seemed from another century, from all other centuries—he was dirty and greasy, his clothes had no style, and he wandered through the city figuring it out: stoplights ("They were Superman's idea. He's the crime-stopper. I'm not sure about the green. Do you know?"), baby carriages ("Rich people use them for their shoats, and poor people are just pretending. They're showing off. It's sad."), etc.

I think of T. and my cock pales in my mind and I foresee gushing come. You laugh! Our functions are funny. So be it. What's the ape that makes that snorting huffing sound with the corners of its lips turned up? The human, I suppose. Dante Alighieri, for instance, at whom few laughed (but some did).

> I was in love with the candor of his odor.
> The clouds roll in from one century to the next.

Did he really know the things I'm only still barely learning (or just glimpse through the noise now and then)? He did. There should be two "learns" (at least). One for data, erudition, and one for "getting it." (He was "wise" to it.) I can see now why he (eleven years younger than me) would have to get mad at me for what I didn't get, for my problems, my blank spots and dim meannesses. But he did put up with me and that makes me proud. My learning is too late. Not that it could have been any different. And of course I put up with him too. Thing is, he didn't need me for long. Didn't want me for long.

But you know what gives me pleasure? That I am his poetry. Poems do have a location and lifespan. They become fossils, shells and imprints of themselves, alive only to the most determined scholars or loving devotees of them. I am closer to the pure origins of his than anyone else will ever be. I am the Way and the Truth.

But the snow is sand in this tedium.

I want another pill. Nurse!

So I talked to Ted that day. Ted always (almost) made me feel better. Thank God for friends with their separate brains.

The day was like dust puffs exploding from the perimeters of a dropped upside-down desk, top smacking the ground.

All the days of the past are like that, all the past. All time is, and here I am stirring it up and adding water and making little shapes out of it.

Mother, I am sorry. But I want the dead ones back. Take me to church.

It is the voice of the human being: talking mud. The clouds roll in from one century to the next. It is a great thing to "speak." But

God preserve me from this stuttering stall. Jeez, the word "being" (as in "human ..."). "I lift my voice in song."

Mornings of smoke, hungover and unwashed, but bright, and avid for T. Little rocking "T." Who pshoots. There's a lot to safely waste.

It's nice the way in old books of poetry some letterpress-printed words are darker than others. Dappled, camouflage. And then some poetry unexpected enough that chances are a stray word will pop-quiz you, like say the word "being" in "human being." I wish there was a way to guarantee that ... It's so preferable to care about the words above oneself, though "easier said than done."

Those who die young don't know what they're missing! It's all worked out.

The older one gets, the more one's drawn to the sky. And of course that's where one is heading. The sky a kind of anti-admonition; a premonition. Not a threat but a promise. Heaven to flow in disintegration that way.

Youth ruled in those days. Every child should have it! To live amidst a population surge like that. What good luck to have our natural self-righteousness supported by the numbers, so the world is ours by rights. To be loathed and courted like royalty by the structure, and to royally scorn and mock the ancient courtiers back. The poverty! The drugs! "Revolution!"

Oh, the drugs. It gives me shivers to think of them and makes my teeth to hurt. Minds: playgrounds; bodies: toys. And all that freaking fear to find and fool with; sudden enthusies turned upside down and inside out. Worms and grubby roots, vaginas gurgling in every bush, eating from your hand. Ruined castles on ruined castles, and it's morning again. I wore a flowered tie sometimes. On a shirt with flowers on it. Velvet pants. Stained and wrinkled but soft as a baby's TV show.

Ted's great homemade magazine, *um*, which T.'d ordered from Kentucky in junior high school and which eventually, in its final issues, was one of the only two magazines where he was ever published while he was alive and writing. Pop art, organic surrealism, and psychedelia.

Retrospectively, all conviction seems poignant.

T. was barely pubescent and off in back provinces for the peak of it, but I was there. Barefoot children giving away flowers on St. Mark's Place. The huge pupils on the LSD'd at 3:00 A.M., Gem's Spa. Artists' parties with acid in the punch. The Rolling Stones and the Velvet Underground and Jimi Hendrix. TV the pixeled vision-mode. The Vietnam War. Ferocity of psychedelic violence, sobbing bewilderment. Big giant screen of what's before your eyes. And then something jumps off it and runs you through.

5

Paul had to go home some time, so he did it drunk. He left Ted near noon, and pressed himself with brisk if wavering concentration back across town toward his neighborhood.

As he foot-stepped wobblily up to his front door his head got clearer, but in fear he acted drunker, distracted. He unlocked, pushed it open one-fingered, and swayed inside. Dead quiet. He swept the door closed and shuffled loudly deeper in. The house seemed eerie again. No one seemed to be home. He climbed the stairs, both hands on the railing. The bedroom door was open and he looked in and it was empty. The house was empty. It was a relief but then a letdown because he'd psyched himself to face her and now she could surprise him at any moment.

He started feeling sentimental about her. She was so simple and sweet, undeserving of his meanness. But then why is everything so goddamned complicated? Aw, if only everyone stayed drunk, then the playing field would be level. Why couldn't she be without him for one night? What difference did it make where he was? Why did she have to make everything a problem?

Then again it was her house, more or less. Her father had given it to them, though she never held that over him. It was the best

Paul'd ever lived, and, furthermore, she yielded to him, accepted his authority in practically everything. She was an angel! Right now, look at that bed, it was beautiful. A headboard, and a comforter so thick with dry aeration it was delicious nakedness itself.

She'd been so innocent when they married, but she'd let him do anything with her! She was happy to make him happy. An angel. Hell, if he'd handled it right she probably would have let him bring T. into bed with them. But T. would have said something terrible.

Paul steered himself across the rug to the liquor cabinet, watching himself, the house silent and disapproving in an essentially indifferent way. He found a nice bottle of wine and tenderly carried the open bottle to the big walk-in closet back downstairs by the front door and went inside to its far corner and sat in the dark among the boots and scarves, a thing he'd never done before, but which he did now smoothly and without hesitation. He smiled a small smile. It smelled comforting like a furry stinky childhood pet. Satin and penises and nipples in the leafy glade.

Paul drank and meditated doubly, in and out of focus. If it weren't for T., he wouldn't have thought to step outside his habits and find this warm dark corner. He was new. Moments of the past two days arose in folds and sheets of dripping pleasure and dissolved through his mind. He was being cuddled by reality, or he'd found a rift in it and had slipped through into the eternal self-cartoon of the creators. Little winged cupids and noble pouting pagan gods voluptuous behind the scenes. Emotions at their origin. This was the reality behind reality, and he was the monkey god, and T. was his master and all was solved because he had his role—to go with T., who understood him and loved him, clearly, to the unknown extent that a human god can love. But Paul intended to go on earning it.

He half hoped his wife would come home and find him here. It might help her to understand. He sure didn't want to be sober when he saw her again.

About his head little cherubs and gamboling mischievous godlets.

"Oh my god, is that her? At the door?! Just think, it's daytime outside. It's a particular hour of a particular year. But I, I have my wisecracking plump tormentors, all pink-skinned, teasing me, dipping and flitting clumsily around me in this garden, nudging, conspiring, all concerned with my dormant penis. Burning steeple of … To burn is so corny. Phosphorescent! Scientific! Who's to say where this breathing goatish room is, really? The sunset is beautiful. And so reliable! Delirium: That would be a great name for a car. It sounds like an element in the periodic table. I love it in here. I will suck that little cherub's teeny cock. What does the tiny spurt from Cupid's penis taste like? Like displaced space. 'The sound of an apple broken in half.' Oh, I am so weak. What's my face turning into? It's concave. But there's no one here for it to scare. I like it, turned inside out and written as music on the wall. Animated cartoons are my exquisite dying thought."

Camera pulls back, through the roof, as a still exposure of Paul in the original shot remains beneath, into oblivion.

***

Mornings of smoke, hungover and unwashed, but bright, and avid for T. Little rocking "T." Who pshoots. There's a lot to safely waste. Avid mornings.

The thing about ……… is that it remains, and is hardly ever dull. Any hurts it causes are unintended, incidental. It feeds.

The curtains were the heaviest things made since the beginning of time and they hung in lovely decorative folds in a plane of substance so near they were hard to identify. Their weave coalesced to open out and be read as glittering informational blur. Information being what can be learned from chaos. The blurred pattern even smelled good.

Paul woke himself up shifting position. He felt pretty queasy, but the main thing was to get out of here, but he couldn't move yet . . . What morning was it? Was it morning? He felt sick. He wanted to leave and find T. He had to find him now and join him.

This I love, to be borne by love. The only person to tell it to is Jesus. My head is a church.

He raised himself to his feet, pushed open the closet door, and there was Carol coming through the front door. She gasped noisily and then went pale and cold looking at him. He crumbled, but became self-righteous almost right away.

"I'm sorry," he said. He was afraid. (Ted would be so large! His good will would be so huge, no one could blame him. But Paul was out of his depth.) He couldn't adjust to her, it was an impassable route. "I'm going," he said.

And at other times he'd undressed her!

She went to the bedroom crying and called her mother. People call their mothers! Dying soldiers scream and moan for them. "Mother." "Ma." When no one else is left, you go to your mother, as impossible as it may be. Even if you have no mother, if she's no one whatsoever, if she's dead, if she's stupid, mean, senile, of another species altogether . . . Do you doubt this? Then you're mistaken. Believe it in this world of shit. Even if she'd rather kill you, or you her. Then you find her and she's someone else. So go to Jesus.

42

Is it possible that one other person on earth can render the rest colorless by his absence? Yes, of course.

***

A few blocks away T. was drinking and writing, intent in his sharp-edged room. The gloomy light through the air-shaft window provoked him. He was a boy always in company, that kind of loner. He was in his laboratory, cooking and sampling, all smeared and greasy, "going for broke," in the grip of it, roaming around in the dimensions.

> A glass of sweetly grainy
> Ovaltine and the grown man
> gone lunk and putrid
> moans to me in tunnels
> through the hills. I swoop
> across the tattered "uh"s
> to him. "Listen.
> Listen, I have a word
> or two for you,
> now buddy, and what
> I thought I spoke came
> from his mouth. 'Tuesday
> Weld,'" he said
> and thereupon we wed.

"What the fuck?" The earthly human motto.

His eye lit on the light. It pissed him off. He picked up a book. It soothed a distracted part of him, but he moved on. Where was the out? He was hungry.

Science and poetry WILL become one.

"Because I know who God is. At first I thought it was 'the way things are.' Now I realize it's our imagination of what made us. As opposed to the Universe.

"But history isn't an accident. From this streaming whirl, what can I tear free. See *through* the eye, not with it, they say. Yawn. How to hold it all at once."

> It's 7:30 A.M. in Benares and there's
> feverish monkey. Think
> of milk, and a young girl
> and her thoughts
> the capillaries feed lengthy tunnels to?!
> Oh so called swollen streams
> in struggling misnomer as if
> there was a will, and ... This
> I offer: this
> ancient vinyl platter known as
> "The Mole
> and What Is Made of It," by
> The Silent Mountain Boys
> to tear free the fair tree
> too so
> the thoughts sing:
> "Nothing's sought"

"No, no, NO, NO, NO," the horrid actor broke down on the set.

"It's funny though, now that I look at those two little things, the things they have in common ... False starts, warm-ups, have the same vague construction of ... statement (setting) (establishing shot); enter person; author addresses person ... And other things . . . Consideration of words, names; quotations. Strange, funny: the form of the shape revealed by its repetition only. If it weren't repeated you'd never realize that the shape was there . . . I'm sleepy."

> In silence of small hums and the ear's own noises
> it is dawn in New York City, each
> unexpected creaking massive from the
> heart of the consoling world to me in quiet
> room. The doves moan and I tune to each
> motion which is a sound and
> drafts of soft grey greeting to present me
> the gifts I brought

He suddenly realized what a good thing it would be to have a cup of coffee and then to pull the cheap fabric of musty print curtains across the grey window and lie naked in the bed underneath the covers with a book, relishing his own tiredness at 6:45 in the morning, light stencilled in borders around the curtains.

He unfolded in slow motion out of his bed, glided around the room, closed the door behind him, watched his feet down the stairs and out into the dawn streets that looked abandoned by revellers at this hour, the dotty refuse evidence of dramas and small crimes and escapades, dimwit pigeons pecking furtively at the remains. There was an aroma of pepper and rotten oranges in the sweet air, air that chilled his elbows and streamed through his nostrils, cooly elating.

He ended up having to walk five blocks to find an open coffee shop, but there he got two containers of sugary pale hot coffee from a miniscule Neanderthal in stained white at the counter.

He carried the coffees back to his room. There he lifted the five books he'd taken from Paul to a little pile beside his bed, stripped, and got under the covers. Rays of sweet color linked his head to the entire city.

> I am italicized and boldly white as I
> plummet to sleep tenderly
> whom the silent beggar rummaging
> envies and the child holds still, thinking me up
> as he gazes at the insect and torn pictures

His ruffled head was densifying inside, and his eyes stung a little, agreeably, as he read, pillows stuffed in the strut of his armpit, hand propping up his grave absorbéd face:

Detach, Invading

> Oh humming all and
> Then a something from above came rooting
> And tooting onto the sprayers
> Profaning in the console morning
> Of the pointing afternoon
> Back to dawn by police word to sprinkle it
> Over the lotions that ever change
> On locks
> Of German, room and perforate
> To sprinkle I say
> On the grinding slot of rye
> And the bandage that falls down
> On the slots as they exude their gas
> And the rabbit lingers that pushes it

To blot the lumber
Like a gradually hard mode
All bring and forehead in the starry grab
That pulverizes
And its slivers
Off bending down the thrown gulp
In funny threes
So the old fat flies toward the brain
And a dent on brilliance

The large pig at which the intense cones beat
Wishes O you and O me
O cough release! a rosy bar
Whose mist rarifies even the strokers
Where to go
Strapping, apricot

6

I t is a pretty picture, R.T. prone on a cot in '71, propping before his face those hinged boards of pure blue spattered with child-style, proud five-pointed white stars. I don't think that image, that scene, as I conjure it up now, is changed by my knowledge of where things were to go. Just a happy picture of dawn. "*Great Balls of Fire*" the white lettering on the book cover reads.

So we're these rips in the fabric of matter, coming out of nowhere to walk down Fifth Avenue and get some fried eggs and coffee. What a translation. $H_2O + \ldots + \ldots = $ Bart Simpson. I can really see it, numbers turn a corner and there's this perverse swarm of shapes and activities named Greta Garbo eating ice cream among a lot of insects and plants and advertisements and everything.

Why have I come to love winter as I have? It's not symbolic, I'm not into my own personal winter. I don't really like winding down and going cold. Well, it's not so bad either. "Rage, rage against the dying of the light"—now that's an idiotic attitude. Talk about sound and fury signifying nothing. Give me a break. But the spidery few-colors of the bricks and dirt, the drained winter sky, the porous curving snow and crackly frost-crust, trunk and branch bark against them in the small daylight, so beautiful! Like white cock slipping into cold pained asshole.

For the last few years, ever since I started napping in the afternoons, I've had these instances of what seems like foreknowledge of it–dying–when I'm waking up. Coming up from dozing–like pulling out of something that clings with suction. Pulling yourself up out of your own undifferentiated substance. You relapse absently back into it temporarily, your mind uncertain and dim, confused, misreading its own content and signs, all the paths in disarray. Everything is grey and tired and unimportant, not oriented. One could go either way. It's dying. I think I've known it without realizing it all along. It's why I always hated sleeping in the day, late afternoon house with no lights on ... But I like it now.

And then when that thing happens where you're tugging yourself away and out, peeling inexorably out of the orbit, and in some vestigial remnant of dream an inappropriate concept is applied to an image, like say you're half aware of trying to figure out the best way to use a grapefruit tool to extract the most nourishment from a way of walking, and then realize you've erred somehow in your reading and linking of the processes and ideas, but are unable to recover the original ... as the challenge fades and you're neutralized–grey-conscious again, solid, sad, alone, and death-tasting, come back awake ...

It is death-tasting, and I'm sure that dying (if it comes peacefully) will be like that, a kind of mild bewildering confusion that this time once and for all subsides back completely, irrevocably, into dispersal of oneself to chaos, inanimate, rather than awakening into order and the confidence of consciousness. It's so typical of nature to give us the preview, start easing and preparing us, making the most efficient use of its means, and sprucing up the inevitable. But the depressing thing is the irreconcilability of this nowhere with how one's spent one's life. Except that the confusion, the senility, the dream and sleep, is the reconciliation itself.

I remember the young girl whom T. talked into coming home with us. She was a poet kid, an intern at the Poetry Project. I swear the poet girls are the most exciting of all girlfriend-types. Thrilled by sex, devoted to it, with great brains, and they're so pretty. There's not a better class of girl to fuck, true feminists of the most rarefied type.

What a pretty memory. We blindfolded her and tied her to a chair. I don't think she'd ever been so excited in her life. The nicest people love a chance to be sexually used without worrying about it.

1. Thank you to capitalism and all those silly companies who try to look cheerful so I'll buy their things.
2. Thank you to those who didn't hoard their sexual possibilities but rendered them freely to me.
3. Thank you to the most shameless pornographers.
4. Thank you to books (music, painting, etc.).
5. In fact, thank you to all distractions.
6. Comfortable shoes.
7. Thank you to dreaming, which is the secret of life and happiness (death).
8. Thank you for chance and accidents, "formlessness" in general (subset of dreaming?).
9. Full-fledged cartoon characters.
10. Praise for me.
11. The people who really think friends and love matter, and don't give up on me even when I'm useless. (Sorry, this is crummy sentimentality. I can't help it.)

"You are in my heart," I thought, to write down, and looked at it. "You are in my heart." Why is that sentence effective? It's sentimental and clichéd but it works right away on me—there's no denying it—actually feeling like affection, like love. And, as T. always said, that's the definition of truth: what works. As if a heart were emotional reality and courage, wherein is given shelter and devoted care.

T. hated sentimentality and he hated anthropomorphizing the universe. He was a scientist, wanting no self-delusion. It was another subject of his, how self-full humans made the whole universe out to be human, to have a human measure, which it isn't and doesn't. But science itself is "what works" too. The truth is what works. It's what there can be the fewest objections to, it's how things are and happen.

A book like a landscape, light between far-off hills, good-smelling air. It was fresh unbroken land that excited him.

Look at this place I got pushed into. An old degenerate in a hospital room. But I can write myself elsewhere. Lying here alone. Traffic in the halls. A kind of nobody to this staff that's seen it all. Fluorescent lights and clean stiff sheets, little push-buttons, electrical voices, flowers, TV, anonymity. It itself is like that confused half-awake state, that half-wit death twin.

7

Paul wove his way through the morning streets' zones and channels of air and pedestriana back toward T.'s hotel. He could taste the tacky way his mouth stank, and there was a bad scraped and itchy feeling in his butt for not having bathed. He licked his lips. Then he did it again in an exaggerated way, like an insane person, just to separate himself from the streaming citizens. Jesus, he was impressionable, but he was happy to be influenced by his new leading man.

He felt a little dizzy and thirsty. He stepped into a deli and bought a big can of beer, two of them, one for T. He went and sat on a bench in Washington Square Park to revive himself with his beer and a cigarette.

The cow is a tree in my buttocks.

The dirty concrete path was too pretty, embarrassingly so. He remembered an Edwin Denby poem he'd memorized once (knew "by heart").

> The sidewalk cracks, gumspots, the water, the bits of
>   refuse,
> They reach out and bloom under arclight, neonlight—

Luck has uncovered this bloom as a by-produce
Having flowered too out behind the frightful stars of night.
And these cerise and lilac strewn fancies, open to bums
Who lie poisoned in vast delivery portals,
These pictures, sat on by the cats that watch the slums,
Are a bouquet luck has dropped here suitable to mortals.
So honey, it's lucky how we keep throwing away
Honey, it's lucky how it's no use anyway
Oh honey, it's lucky how no one knows the way
Listen chum, if there's that much luck then it don't pay.
The echoes of a voice in the dark of a street
Roar when the pumping heart, bop, stops for a beat.

It was about nighttime but still ... "By-produce!" And the quiet,
the defenselessness of it (titled "The Silence at Night"), renewing
rhymes, itself an example of its subject. "Flowered too out behind
the frightful ..." It seemed like it should be set to music ... And the
unprepossession of it, the humility of it, like a net, a web, but the
scale of which can't be gauged ...

A stringy-haired guy in dirty rumpled clothes and wearing a
backpack going by looked Paul in the eye and muttered something
under his breath and Paul double-took when he was five feet past.

Spontaneously, inspired, Paul coughed out a sharp undertone,
"Ey!" The guy slowed up a little bit and Paul realized he was supposed to get up and walk with him, so he did, yanking along his
beers, tearing the bag, but magically capturing the cans before
they fell.

He choked, "Acid?"

"Windowpane."

"How much is it?"

"Three bucks a hit."

"…Um gimme three."

The dealer pointed, and they dropped down onto a bench and Paul dug a wadded ten-dollar bill from his pants pocket in exchange for three tiny transparent drug-sliver plaques, like doll fingernails, and a one-dollar bill into which he folded them.

"Have a nice day." The drug man smiled before sliding down the bench a little and getting up and walking off. A couple of cops were swaggering intrusively down the path and Paul's heart clenched, but they passed on by, one glancing at him a little contemptuously.

There was all this gurgling and oooing of pigeons coming from the grass behind him. He tuned to it, and it swelled in a warm overflow, a nice sound, like a mother's voice, or the happy baby, like sex, like wetting your pants. Like he couldn't differentiate it from himself. He carefully, surreptitiously, slid the bill pac, little green origami envelope, out of his pocket, unfolded it, and looked at the clear square punchclips on it. They didn't seem to have defined edges, and looking at them had a weird effect on the inside of his mouth, like a conditioned reaction, as if he'd thought of something sour. It triggered a release of saliva, and gave his body a surprised spacy feeling like that moment of an injury before anything actually hurt. There was the start of a hardon in there too. He anticipated shivering. Just from looking at those little square acid flecks.

He put the drugs back away and popped the top and took a big gulp from his foamy imposing green and bronze 16 oz. Ballantine Ale. That was comforting, improving. Acid in his pocket. It made him feel like he'd just come into an inheritance. He drank some more beer, and smiled a little.

He remembered something T.'d been going on about: emotions. They're all nonsense, he'd said. People make such a big deal about them, congratulating themselves, acting as if there's something profound, *worthy* about them. How pathetic. What are they? Biological reflexes, like sex. You hate and fear threats to your well-being; get angry at … disturbances; love nourishment, pleasure, relief. What's all the sloppy big deal about them? Pathetic human self-congratulation, over-weening, foolishness. Jesus Christ, how bad off do you have to be to want credit for your fucking emotions? There's no *value* to them apart from their biological function of self-protection. They're not goddamned standards of meaning, proofs of worth! Fucking hippies. And it's so funny the way they're exploited by the advertisers, manipulated by cheap "artists," politicians, and con men of all types … T. would flout them. T. would defy the tyranny of "feelings" and their sad and dimwit partisans.

Paul drank some more beer. It was reviving. He had an urge to drop one of those acid flecks onto his tongue right now. Yes? No? Yes? No? No.

He had a moment of fear remembering his wife, took another long slug of beer, thinking of T. in that hotel room. And then that the room was expensive and T. wasn't going to be having any money. Maybe he could just get the kid a cheap apartment over on the Lower East Side.

"It's Paul," he called through the door. He was holding some yellow freesias he'd bought on the way over.

"What? I'm asleep."

"I know. Just let me in …" and in a few seconds the door opened, "I'm tired too, really sleepy too." Paul walked inside. "I couldn't stay at the house … I just gotta crash. Go on back to bed …"

"Ah uhmm," and the boy turned back around.

Paul joined him in bed by the blue, starred book and listened to him fall back asleep and then a few minutes later fell asleep himself.

They woke up late in the day and took the acid.

The idyll of the cheap hotel room, pencil and paper pad, doughnuts, streaky window, sex. Fear of looking in eyes (and then they sadden). Cheap portable typewriter and the burnt, charred, purple-looking letters of the alphabet it smacked into the white, fibrous paper. You could almost smell them—the words—they smelled like burning teeth, the fumes from dentists' drilling. Rich and hot and deathly innocent. There should be a law against something looking so pretty, because it was a crime the way they promised so much. No, no, no, no: It's fine. Paul and T. stopped talking because it complicated and confused things too much, and the sound was ominous and inappropriate; they gestured and wrote notes and laughed too uncontrollably. Laughing looked grotesque on T., so unnatural. Then a word escaped and started everything again. T. was furious and they both cried, trying not to make too much noise, but the effort just doubled the fear. T. had a Robert Crumb comic book. Through the airshaft, far away, a radio was playing "Just My Imagination" by the Temptations.

The trick was to remember you could change direction. Gradually the mouth got very big, like popular. The senses, the means of perception, they were plenty after all. Who needs x-ray vision?

Sense of the room as a compartment in the all, the local mercifully sealed off from the endless, a shelter from it but full of leaks and seepages, like tendrils: soft voices, smells . . . And people themselves—one oneself—similarly, a kind of shelter, a reduction/interpretation of the activities—the expressions—of "energy" . . . In that sense "life" as usually thought of was negative, a reduction . . . A blind little fungus, parasite, on boundless, and by that token meaningless, reality. Life, to the extent that it individuated itself . . . that it conceived of itself as separate (from reality: the "dead").

56

The trails that everything leaves. Eyes in action, nerves, brain. Or is it "everythings leave?" What, wait, I'm (confused). You can trace back to my brain, and thence to penis. Which evacuates liquid waste and is the … Down there with the intestinal exit for solid waste. Where does the time go? It goes into airless places, taking your breath for its scuba gear.

A touch: "merge" … ? Mouth to nipple, etc. "Wouldn't it be booful if we could juth run together into one gwate big bwob?" Let your goosey flesh feed you: smells, views, eroticism, etc. I is a projector. Lost powers of speech. Everything but everything was sex, mental hurt, and it was hard to take. Which did you want to keep, this or the rest? Now you may cry.

Metallic taste.

But Christ, the thrill of being with this boy with whom he could do anything, and the boy not only allowed it (whether or not the boy'd go along with it) but was smart and similar enough so that Paul knew he was understood … It was love, the "stuff" of love, as petty as that may be.

"I HATE WORDS." But there's no substitute. They're my life, they're my wife. I FUCK MYSELF. Oh Christ, don't think "wife." Oh shit.

T.'s head is streaming like a horse. Those nostrils. The red and pink where they cup against his face. Paul's eyes won't stop that surprised watering. T.'s shoulder blades were deers' hooves.

"your lips are indeed a disaster of alienated star-knots"

The taste of his unwashed, uncut dick as Paul sucked it and T. listened to the Velvet Underground on headphones stuck in a cheap portable record player he'd borrowed from the desk clerk … Paul was his appliance too and got into it like a baby curled up sucking for his own pleasure but subordinate to Him who hardly noticed as if it practically wasn't a person to Him, but purely a tool. Paul almost lost his mind it made him so happy still, and the chains went on linking in either direction . . . And the taste! And his own cock rousing, to put it mildly, from its muddle of crotch smell as he did it, stars in his eyes, skin moistening with the opening-out, every hole, pore, a socket, as nature abhors a vacuum, he almost shit his pants . . . Jerked himself off while he sucked the cock, and—like fireworks—. . . hypnagogic visions . . . The moisture at every turn. Shivers . . .

T. would also go so soft and sweet on him like the dawns he liked so much.

That dawn they lay side by side describing the limping fauns and children fading from where they'd crept and sauntered forth with the new light in their minds in the small hotel room.

"Maybe LSD is our compensation for these grotesque brains," he said.

8

Two days later they got up and went and waited in line for a *Village Voice* across the street from Village Cigars, with its big tomato-red sign like the heart of town, among the manhole covers and happy doughnut smells of Sheridan Square, where the first copies of the weekly paper were delivered to the traffic-island newsstand. They sat in the exposed little wedge-shaped park alongside and marked the classifieds for apartments. By mid-afternoon Paul'd rented one for T. on the south side of East 6th Street between First and Second Avenues, second floor rear, for $90 a month.

The apartment was one square room facing out the back of the building where two windows opened onto a rickety fire escape over a half-paved lot with a solitary tree. There was a little kitchenette patched onto the room in the opposite direction, and a small bathroom with a shower stall past that. The light was bad, the roaches numerous, and the style a cheap, ugly "renovation" of an old tenement: mouldings removed, wallboard nailed on, and fixtures replaced. The price was right though. There were still fresh speckles and drips of white latex where the place had just been painted.

They furnished it with a futon, a couple of hardware store clip-on aluminum hood lamps, some candles for temporary light, and a bottle of Wilson's whiskey. They made an appointment with the phone company, and took the lease up to Con Edison on 14th Street to order gas and electricity.

Paul knew the neighborhood well and he called it the Lower East Side—rather than the East Village, which he regarded as cheesy media/marketing language.

The Fillmore East rock concert hall, a beat-up former movie house with its big marquee, was right down 6th Street on the far corner at Second Avenue. On the near—east—side of the avenue and between 5th and 6th Streets was a handy storefront where you could get paid $5 to lie on a cot and donate a pint of blood. Just north at St. Mark's Place (8th Street east), in Gem's Spa all-night news/tobacco/candy/fountain/ice cream, you could find your 25¢ Bugler or Top loose tobacco and tubs of fresh Breyer's ice cream (vanilla with its little flecks of the bean). This was the corner of the neighborhood's carnival midway block—St. Mark's between Second and Third Avenues—where runaways proffered their pacifist flowers and panhandled barefoot, as stoned as possible, also around the clock. On that block too was the little storefront East Side Book Store, which carried all the radical and counter-cultural pamphlets including New York poetry, and, further down, the big well-stocked St. Mark's Books. Just up from the corner on Second Avenue, St. Mark's Movie Theater showed second-run double features for $2.

For physical nourishment there was:

Ratner's Dairy Restaurant right by the Fillmore, open all night, with mushroom barley soup that came with a basket of delicious bright-yellow onion rolls and sweet butter; or

the B & H up a block, with its chewy, soft crackle-crust challah bread, and hot borscht lumpy with beans and giant vegetable chunks; or

Veselka's with its pierogies (square dumplings—boiled or golden-fried—stuffed with cheese or mushrooms or potatoes or spinach or meat . . .) with sour cream and apple sauce and sweet, gooey spoonfuls of sauteed onions, at 9th Street and Second; across the avenue from

the Orchidia, for chicken marsala and spaghetti al dente and garlic bread on special occasions; and a block north from

the Ukrainian National Home of goulash; or

the kosher Second Avenue Deli—good big hamburgers or four-inch-high pastrami or corned beef on rye, bowls of pickles, and Dr. Brown's Celery Tonic, at 10th Street . . .

Opposite the deli, across Second Avenue, stood the 18th-century St. Mark's Church, where the Episcopalian priest let the poets meet and use the mimeo machine to publish. Raw's Drink, where the readings were held, was right there too, between 9th and 10th Streets down from the church. The liquor store was across from the church, or you could get codeine Romilar at the drugstore on the same block. Heroin for the hard cases was three blocks east on Avenue B (after the numbered avenues passed First, going east the lettered avenues went from "A" to "D" before hitting the highway and then the river). Grass and acid were everywhere.

Both the poets were still wasted from the hotel-room acid two nights before and then putting together the apartment all day, so, early in the evening, after pizza and some whiskey, they crashed.

They were awakened in the morning by the neatly pressed over-cologned Con Ed man in his blue uniform arriving to switch on the power and stove gas.

T.'d never had an apartment before. He was surprised by his happiness that morning, his own bare whole place, New York City, in the toned-down, cool light that staggered in from the back alleys.

"It seems like I just stepped from my bedroom in Covington, where I lived since I was five in that nowhere tract house run by my hard-ass ma, into a . . . *Star Trek* closet, a transporter, to New York City, where no one can tell me what to do . . . I didn't expect it to happen so . . . directly . . . It's very great. I might just do it again."

"What?"

"Leave. It's such a great feeling."

It seemed like T.'d probably like to be alone so Paul said he had to be going. They were expecting him at work. But first he ran out for a package of boric acid powder and an aluminum drip coffee pot, a shiny yellow and red can of strong El Pico coffee, waxy white and blue carton of milk, bright yellow box of sugar.

The colors and splashy brand names brightened the room and seemed to oppose the roaches. He started the coffee brewing and then poured the boric acid roach killer behind the cabinets and appliances in the kitchen. He drank a cup of coffee with T. and went to kiss him. T. didn't respond but thanked him for his help and Paul gave him $10 again and left nicely though his heart was beating too hard.

T. took his coffee mug outside and sat halfway down the steep steps leading up to the building's entrance. Citizens were hurrying to work all groomed and preoccupied. Skinny young T. sat vaguely distracted, feeling stoked but calm, and watched. He was wearing soft bell-bottom jeans that were purple in longways pencilmark-thin fuzzy red and blue stripes, and a pocketed steel-blue T-shirt, worn-out to the point of holes at the seams, his ratty, thatched, not-too-long, vaguely insane-looking hair setting him apart.

"Johnny's in the basement mixing up the medicine / I'm on the pavement thinking bout the goverment..." Man, he needed some music. Had to pick up a little cheap record player, or at least a radio. A few good records would make up for any shortcomings in his new apartment.

It was positively futuristic to be a citizen of this here now center of the world, named so ultramodernly for old York.

T. wondered if he could write about it, his mind turning from Dylan to Nixon. Nixon the opposite of Dylan, right? Does that make them creators of each other? What could you do with that? Was there anywhere to go with that? Dylan's name looked like Dylan too. Warm lanolin, island, dying, groves of wood. "My arms are warm." They both have hanging noses and tense mouths. Richard Nixon—cross-eyed, his tight downturned lips where the spit leaks out at the corners. What if you switched their names? "Richard Nixon" in a workshirt singing with civil rights workers, "Dylan" thrilling to say "kike" and "nigger." Well that doesn't really go anywhere, except to stretch your mind a little, and any attention to Nixon was too much attention. Intellectuals liked to think about him. But what could you do with that idea of opposites making each other if the opposites were Dylan and Nixon? You'd have to be a Hindu. What was it in the way minds worked that made everything divide into opposites? Probably DNA itself, genes, "life," which wants to—*wants to* physically, as everything is physical, the way water *wants to* be a solid at temperatures below 32° F.—reproduce and preserve itself, as "opposed to" cease. (Sex, sex again.) People—or "civilized" people anyway—find it hard to muster fellow-feeling for, say, a rock, or to consider themselves as comparably "dead," despite their equally mechanical–chemical, chemanical–operation. Sex. Maybe when cloning would be common, when DNA of the long "dead" would be used to make perfect new versions of original human beings, people would come to fear death no more than a paper cut … (Though the tendency to preserve one's state in respect to motion–inertia–is a physical law of its own, but then so is entropy …) Except wouldn't the *personality* then, the *character,* see itself as separate–opposed–still, and want to preserve itself? But doubtless ways'll be found for recording personality and copying it into fresh human media as well … So is this materialist? Yes and no; human="intelligent"–which is to say constructed so as to find (/create) patterns in existence–"insights" which necessarily conflict with the materialist.

T.'s eye fell on an oblong of sidewalk in front of the stoop and he decided to look at it.

He got up and took his coffee cup inside and then came back out and went for a walk.

9

T. wanted Paul to take him to where the poets gathered, but it never went well, even when Ted was there. One night a couple of months after T. hit town, Paul brought him to a collating party at Jane Connor and Joe Storch's house on St. Mark's Place. Jane and Joe edited and published a literary magazine. It was an elegant mimeo called ~ P~ or *Space Pee*.

The room was so thick with grass smoke it seemed it might condense and coagulate on you. A couple of sexless breathers in faux-chivalry and beads tinkled from the stereo. The poets dressed either in peasant corduroy and faded cotton, or pop star suede and satin, flaring velvet, itsy-bitsy flower prints. They were grad students, small-time drug dealers, bookstore clerks, artists' assistants: eyeglasses and no haircuts, soft waists, pimples. But they were young and smart and many of them had produced memorable poems. They flopped on the two overstuffed armchairs, a sofa and some kitchen chairs, or stood among them around a large table. The table was covered with inches-high stacked rows of the pages of *Space Pee* #3. The cover of this issue was a high-art cartoon of a monkey mixed with a table lamp in Kokomo City.

Somebody said, "Hey, you know what I just saw? That 'glamour' comes from 'grammar.'"

"Always has, always will."

"But will it play in Hollywood? I think not."

"There was Arthur Miller."

"'Grammatica' meant 'learning,' or 'lettered,' and then in the Middle Ages the learnèd were expected to know the magic arts, and 'grammar' became 'glamour,' like *enchanting*…"

"Do you think it could be possible to use your brains to increase your sex appeal?"

"Don't let's be greedy."

"Yeah, lit majors are already the sexiest girls, and they *prefer* poets."

"That's true."

The room was six boys to two girls.

T. wanted to contribute. "Look, granted, it can't be denied, literature departments are nice stables of pussy for you poet-boys, but aren't females a little passé in the fuck arena by now?"

That was a mental ditch; the room parted. Then it resumed, retaining a zone of creepy tense nothing for a little bit. T. seemed oblivious. It was almost as if he were drunk, the way he behaved.

Somebody said, "We ought to have a benefit carnival for *Space Pee* and let people pay to throw baseballs at R.T. Man, we could make a fortune."

"Hey, shut up," T. said. "No, I'd do that. Put on some clown makeup, write "poet" across my chest, scream at the marks, 'So whaddaya think of *that*, scumbags?! Check me, squares, you silly dicks.' That'd be great. Let's do it … Put me in the kissing booth too and you could really clean up."

"… when Katy and I saw Neil Young in January."

"Yeah, how was it?"

T. broke in, "It was OK, but let me tell you I had a really good shit this morning and that was better. On the one hand, a deluded hippie doing Bob Dylan with his nuts froze off. But a good shit to scrub your guts and give you a fantastic little rubdown at your asshole too? No contest."

"Listen man, cool it. Or go away. Or get your nose busted."

"You want to fight? I'll pulverize you, white boy."

And then he giggled, all hyper, outside with Paul.

"Pansies," he said, "Woo hoo. What a rush."

"They're just going to stop telling me when they're getting together."

"We can always find out from Ted."

"But why do you want to go if you're just going to act like that?"

"They provoke me, they push me into it! I can't just stand there…"

"They provoke *you*?"

"Yeah! I'm not blind!"

"You're not blind."

"No I ain't," T. said. "Maybe you would prefer to help me buy a hamburger?"

"Uh, uh huh… As broke as I am I guess I would… We could get a pint of Wilson's and take a couple of burgers back to your place."

"Bingo. Thanks man."

10

All the mornings of a lifetime, like pills taken.
"You people of the future / How I hate you / You are alive and I'm not" And the kangaroo face pulls back a corner of the dawn and laughs. Padgett and mortality—would make a dandy study.

More of This Light

This evening's clear light and light blue pink look like the Penguin edition of *Elective Affinities*, but something was missing there, my stomach is nervous, Goethe I should have said, and the deep green of the fields was glowing an inwardly deeper green the blacktop wound through and on which I sailed along, with just the first hint of feeling that I might someday accept not being here anymore, if only the light would stay this way.

Well, that was evening not morning. I've mixed up spring and fall a few times too.

68

Once they get everything copied onto computer, somebody ought to do an anthology of "light" incidence. It must be the most popular word in 20th-century English-language poetry. Why? Did Einstein do that? Or is it because everything became "everyday" and light is the most poetic thing of the "everyday?"

Of course to die is normal. Often it's possible to look around and see all this "life" as just more roiling of matter. Really, we are not apart from the moon or helium or photons (speaking of light). It must all be an intelligence. How else could we be intelligent if we aren't grown from intelligence? That's self-evident. God is just good science!

My room in the hospital. One vase of dried-up tulips. Earlier I spent five minutes circling it like a movie camera. It was thrilling. I moved with my legs in short, smooth-as-I-could steps with my eyes fixed on the crinkling purple and white (originally red and white) and pale green (the leaves) flowers. The first feeling was of beauty, the second was of struggling to understand what was the significance of this particular changing view of the delicate crisp flowers. I was struggling to get the moment as I made it. I got kind of giddy. "A terrified faun shows his two eyes / And bites the red flowers with his white teeth. / Stained and reddened like old wine, / His lips burst in laughter under the branches."
  You can see why a man might welcome delirium! And who wouldn't?! And why on earth not!?! On earth, I ask you! Why on earth not!?!

You get old too, and in many moods dying seems minor, obvious, not frightening. It's like paying off all your debts or something— death and taxes!—it might be costly, but it's the way of things, and it neatly disposes of the large weight of many burdens. When you're due, you deal with it.

I have one friend who visits and gives me her nipples and breasts to suck and sink my face into. She wears a tube top under an open blouse and pulls up the undershirt and bends over my face pretending to be fiddling with something on the bedstand across the bed from her. (They don't let us close the doors to our rooms when we have visitors.) Her breasts dangle plumply across my face and I am a baby king. I like her to do it just before she leaves so I can go in the bathroom afterward and finish up. She brought me some naked Polaroids of herself too.

Some people like me as the growling old scam artist. I can do that. Though I've actually become pretty civilized, if I do like my little whiskeys and pills.

A funny thing about Him was how much he loved the countryside, woods, unsettled places. That was uncool in New York among the poets in those days (though some were succumbing to Zen beat nature). They were fans of newsstands and movie houses and coffee counters, cocktails and crowds and cigarettes. They were flâneurs, but T. loved the drives into the fields and woods.

***

Paul rented a car and took the boy for a drive up along the Hudson. T. could never get enough of those rides away from the city. In the corner of the front seat of the spacious new-smelling Plymouth Fury, T. leaned against the door and gulped in the streaming air, squinting his watering eyes.

"Let's just find a little ville and walk. Maybe one with a bookstore, and then walk out past the edge of town."

"But could you refrain from writing 'Shit on God' on the park benches?"

"Look man, they ask for it ... I *should* stop saying 'God' though ... The funniest thing happened the other day. I was home and I saw this bird land on the railing of the fire escape outside the window. It was a mourning dove. It was really close. It had just stopped by, not like a person visiting, but a bird on its way to somewhere else ... And being so close it was really detailed and ... clear-cut. Hyper-real. Charismatic, you could say. Did you ever notice those little black marks, deep black tiny streaks, like horizontal cedillas, behind its eyes, and the little blurred wedges at the top of its neck on each side, and then the scattered cup-shapes on its wings? Birds do seem more like works of art than any other thing in nature. And I was looking at it, its pink legs, stiff walk, small head with the bright eyes, chesty torso, soft grey-brown coat with iridescent areas at the top of the breast, and I realized that it reminded me of someone I knew. You don't know her. She was an old schoolteacher of mine. I had a crush on her even though her head was so small. And I got this feeling of a dove and a person just being the slightest variations of each other, birds and humans, animals and humans, period. And then I let myself feel like one myself, a bird. And I did for a second. But mainly it was the realization that we're not that far apart, we're hardly different at all, considering the range of things. Except that maybe birds are better."

"Does that have something to do with God?"

"No. God is dead. Though for practical purposes, he just bumped his head a little. After all, people can't smell him decomposing because he's just an idea. But then so is everything, right?

And that God idea is never going to die anyway, because what it really means is … 'what is …' 'how things are.' Though in fact it'll stay around as all the shit superstitions and self-congratulations and false consolations too, most likely as long as people do … Scientists love their numbers and equations and computations so much as a refuge from doubt and fear. They think math is dependable, that it's secure, but numbers are ideas too. The truth is 'what works.'

"I mean—true, numbers and science have consequences, and it's their reliability that makes that possible, but, first, the advances are only accessible to, or possible in, minds that can accomodate the unexpected; and, second, the aesthetic and psychological remains the same. It's just the physical environment that changes, and the changes are just more details added to our self-portrait. The 'consequences' already exist in some sense. It's not like we, with the numbers and science, really create anything; we just happen upon it in pursuit of our brains. Anyway, all those material advances are really luxuries, enjoyed by the rich … I know it's kind of silly of me to write 'Shit on God.' But I have to. It's my job. And 'God will forgive me. It's his trade.'"

"You're silly."

"I am so silly."

T. felt embarrassed by how happy he was. The car whipped along the Henry Hudson, then the Sawmill River Parkway up to the Taconic. The heady branchings of the trees along the highways were blurred, misted with buds and the palest green first leaves. Some cherry trees and dogwoods bloomed in pink and white, and daffodils and dandelions and crocuses were out in places too. The grass was bright and clumpy. Deer showed up here and there.

T. and Paul lay in the grass up the bank from the Hudson.

"I want to … I want to …"

"Well?"

"Look at us here," said T., "how my skin is quilted, dented, imprinted, there, and speckled, from the sod, you're a twenty-seven-year-old man, I'm a teenage boy, I need to piss, I'm kind of itchy, you're a little worried …"

"I'm not worried …"

T: "Did you ever try to fuck something not human?"

"Huh? Uh … Yes. A little pony."

"They are cute, the little ones."

"I was drunk and showing off."

"I tried to fuck a tree once. I was lonely."

"I never tried to have sex with a plant."

"Plant? It's more like a building. Not to mention its penis-like aspects. But mostly it was something that had a hole in it at about the right size and position. Though it was kind of cool to be naked in the woods. I was a little nervous though."

"I bet."

"… The other day I was trying to think of what was the best thing about America and what I came up with was drug stores with soda fountains. Motels, but they're more worldwide, I think. But a little drug store with a magazine rack and some stationery and school supplies, lots of toiletries of course, then a soda fountain counter and two or three booths where you can get a grilled cheese sandwich and a bowl of tomato soup and a chocolate malted. Romilar with codeine!"

"What about movie stars?"

"All you think about is movie stars."

"Lana Turner."

"Oh Christ, be a man."

"But Lana Turner goes with soda fountains."

"Lana Turner goes with silly queens."

"If Tuesday Weld came over that hill, you'd wilt like a leaf."

"Are you kidding me? I'd jump her so fast your head would spin. She would go for me in a jumbo manner. I'd stare at those bare bare wide-set eyes of hers until I was sick to my stomach. The way those puckery lips still seem to move like precision instruments! What a person."

The rural vista with its river and trembling greenery, dappled and detailed and fragrant—deep volumes of landscape in basins of sky—was a world of pleasure, a wall-less room of love.

Bugs crawled on the poets' necks.

T. said, "I swear, the countryside, very little obvious human interference, it just kills me, I almost can't take it it's so good."

11

Today my old friend Max came to visit me and he was all distraught. He's just my age but he hasn't mentally caught up with how old he is. He thinks of himself as being who he was five or ten years ago, or sometimes even twenty or thirty years. (It's true: When you get past a certain age, things do start going in reverse, taking you back to infancy. You even go through reverse adolescence, where you're all disconcerted at the changes taking place in you, only now it's negative and slow motion, losses of capacities . . .) He paced around my bed all messed up and frowning, appalled at having gotten a glimpse of himself. I had to laugh, but I could understand. His innocence wasn't innocent anymore. And he is fifty-three. Me, I'm more like thirty-five except for when I see a picture of myself or stay on my feet too long or try to remember what I did yesterday.

He'd been walking over here from the bus stop in the glaring sunshine, glancing around, half-consciously watching the passersby coming and going, when it dawned on him that he was mentally discarding them all, as if they were trash. He was looking at everyone to measure them against himself, which was bad enough, but he was doing it just to find something inferior about them to make himself feel good. He was shocked to suddenly see that he'd become that way, that he was that dried up and petty.

"Max," I told him, "it doesn't necessarily mean you're a creep. It's just insecurity."

"I don't want to be insecure either. You mean I'm never going to grow up? It's disgusting, man. What's the use? I used to look at people and be curious about them, interested in them. I respected people. Now I mentally trample them so I can feel superior!"

"It's just a bad day, a bad mood ..."

"I'm always in a bad mood! Every once in a while I can get a little flush of good will, of fellow-feeling, if I'm alone, or talking to someone appealing—someone less burnt-out than me ... But probably I'm just glad for a chance to identify with them so I can feel like a good person myself! ... Or a movie! People in movies can make me feel like a nice guy! But I'm a scumbag! Maybe I always was to some degree, but now it's taken over. I'm fucked! It's no good not to be who you think you are! ... And then I think, 'How can a writer be like this?' Does it mean I have to avoid certain subjects, or ... contexts, to avoid having it fuck my writing? I'm fucked. It's all over. I see why Hemingway killed himself."

"Hemingway?"

"Yeah. But the point is, what do you do when what you value about yourself, what you think you respect in yourself, is gone? There's nothing good about just *continuing*. You're fucked. And you can't go back, you can't be a virgin again. You can't go back once you've really seen yourself. Forget Hemingway. How about the Jews who survived the camps who ended up killing themselves? Yeah, sometimes it's 'survivor's guilt,' but I think more often it's not being able to get back innocence about the goodness of life, of *themselves*. They've seen how survival comes at the expense of others, they know how they're borne by the bodies of those that died in horrible suffering, their own people they outfought or cheated to survive, and there's no going back …"

"You're thinking too much … But you know, listen to me, there is the Church. Catholicism gives you your virginity back over and over."

"I can't do that, Paul, I can't afford that."

"What do you mean?"

"Well, I'd really have to give up everything about myself to join a religion. I mean, it's not an option."

"It could be OK to give up everything about yourself. It could be fantastic."

"Hmm. No, please … I don't have the patience for this. Sorry …" And he changed the subject. I think he didn't want to accidentally insult me.

He didn't want to be proselytized. I'd never make a Catholic pitch to someone who didn't want it. But it's a shame because I have a lot of good ideas on the subject.

I mean so what if the whole thing is a big psychological trick that you play on yourself? "Rational" people do that in lots of small ways all the time. That's how I look at it. But intellectuals are just automatically prejudiced against religion. It's their loss. The Church is so pretty! And it's no different from athletes psyching themselves up for the game or everyone's little rituals for putting themselves in the right frame of mind. Confession, too! What a brilliant idea! And then you do penance and everything's fresh and new again. If you can believe it. God is good! And you get to pray to a woman! God has a mother!

Consider all the brilliant believers throughout history. Actually there aren't that many. The Church is really for the "little people."

It's helped me through some horrible things.

And it reminds you to try and be compassionate all the time too.

But mostly it's a consolation.

I mean look at Max's misery. Wasn't it really a kind of self-involvement? His self-hatred itself enabled by a kind of pathological self-involvement? Wouldn't it be relieved by compassion and service? By an admission and acceptance of his imperfection, and a scheduled self-humbling?

And it's so pretty!

I know, I suppose, that in a way it's willed ignorance, that it's to say that there are some things one doesn't want to know about. One calls some things Satan and one doesn't want to listen too long to Satan.

And what about my poems of orgies and drunkenness? But I believe God understands. We fell from innocence, but it was worth it to God to have us have the choice to love and praise Him. Not that God really needs to be praised, but He's in me and I need it! But really it's too complicated. I'm not a priest. I submit to priests. Incense and heart-breaking obscene flowers.

I admit it's hard to maintain. It's hard to submit at times. There's actually a kind of penance for my arrogance, kind of a self-flagellation, just in accepting the way the word "God" is thrown around so easily by priests. A person should really not ever say that word without specific accompanying preparation. To say the word is like making a judgement that has critical consequences, like presiding over a criminal trial. It should be done with care. I mean just the phrase "God's Word" is hard for me to accept (because who is qualified to recognize it?), and it pops up everywhere in the Church.

But then, also, all the rules and traditions and controversies are marvelous and absorbing in themselves, as pattern and narrative, like movies or baseball or bird-watching.

And all those paintings. The Annunciation! The way Gabriel's wings are rainbow colors in all those lovely cramped medieval paintings, and Mary is interrupted reading to be told she'll be the mother of God.

St. Theresa. Dante. Simone Weil. Anne Porter! Thomas Merton. Apart from the not too reliable society of artists, I have no society except the Church—one that's been generating beauty and information across thousands of years, including exquisite Books of Hours, St. Augustine's *Confessions*, all the history and intrigues of the Vatican, Baron Corvo, the Italian Renaissance . . . Not to mention Jesus Christ! Yay! Peace.

Probably best of all is that you're given someone—the priest— that actually cares about the state of your soul, and with whom you can talk about it and work on improving it. Where else are you going to get that? *Not* from a psychiatrist . . .

That and the existence of a true model for behavior, Jesus Christ . . .

It makes me so happy to have it and to surrender to it. And that's all that's asked of one, really. It's only as complicated as one makes it.

You know, they keep this ward locked.

I wonder if it'd be fun to be a missionary. You'd think the pagans'd corrupt the missionary, which I guess has been known to happen, at least in literature. But I'm already corrupt. I'd enjoy talking them out of all their little gods in exchange for the one big God I'd bring. Of course God is three Himselves, but it's not the same thing.

I guess I've come a long way from T. He probably wouldn't acknowledge me now. He'd think I was a silly, weak old man. He always did. But people don't really connect with each other on this earth except when they're drunk or children. Saying "I love you" is just a way of fooling your brain for a little cheap relief, a kind of mild Ecstacy. Isn't it? No. There's a feeling the word "love" describes, and there are people who always evoke it.

Why are soap containers so beautiful? The packaging, I mean. Brillo, Ivory, Tide, Comet. It can't be a coincidence. But the thing I really love to see, that gladdens my heart, is a thick stand of empty two-liter plastic generic soda bottles pressed against each other on the floor. The soft gleamings, the complexity of the light, the humility, the blue labels, the uniform bottle shape in the random blob of the clustering...

Lie in bed and surrender to gravity. But it doesn't want me.

Never mind. I can't believe the sky outside, this dawn. I can feel a tiny chill of it too even in here. I can see the sky and a soft faraway slit of sunlight on brick through a corner of exposed window. The hospital interferes with the sky, it processes it, but somehow there's enough of the original left to make me glad to be alive.

Let me tell you what he looked like. It's been proposed that perhaps the body is the best image of the mind. He was very thin, as teenage kids will be. He was a rampaging adolescent. His nostrils were as scanty as teeny chipped seashells. His face was stretched downwards a little to one side, like its tension released, barely detectible, because he'd had Bell's Palsy one morning. An eyelid hung slightly lower than the other. The mildly thuggish, rotten-gene effect of that was a cool counterpoint to the intelligence in his face, eyes. His long legs, which only showed hair below the knees, were always scuffed and abraded. He never went to a bar-ber, but cut his hair himself. It was thick, and when he arrived in

New York it was long, but then he cut it all off and it was short and ragged. He usually had a couple of little pimples on his face, around the nose. His complexion was pale. You could easily see each of the widely separated hairs on his upper lip and on his chin and the little strip down along the edge of his jaw. He didn't need to shave more than twice a week. His cock was average length, maybe a little longer than average, uncircumcised, and quite thick. It slanted a little to his left and curved upwards when erect. He had at most four or five thin dark chest hairs. His nipples were unexceptional, medium-sized and flat. He was more or less shaped like a fish. That's ridiculous, why did I say that? Maybe it's because thinking of him naked, his cock especially, makes me think of the belly of a fish, something so exposed, strange, out-of-context, illegal—as well as pale and throbbing. His face had the beauty of human undifferentiation, of healthy youth. His eyes were deep-set and his nose was medium length and thin and turned up. His teeth were a little crooked, endearing when he smiled, which wasn't often.

It is an advantage he had: to be so close to his own childhood. But that's another similarity to advanced age. Old men forget the names of their children but not what happened that day in the fourth grade.

How close is the imagination to reality? Close enough: Even reality is not like reality. That's why poetry beats philosophy.

12

*We are not physicists nor metaphysicians: we must be
Egyptologists. For there are no mechanical laws between
things, nor voluntary communication between minds.*
                                        —Gilles Deleuze

S lobbering mud and rubies. Cities without evenings.
I've been trying to get what I can out of Mallarmé the last
few days. I don't read French. I just go with my stack of translations and their footnotes and commentaries. Mallarmé loved
Baudelaire and so do I—and so did T. Mallarmé is harder to get
through the language barrier though. But then I realized all poetry is translation. My understanding of him has its reality. It's legit-
imate. T. told me about Kurt Gödel, way back then.

"That gutter drain [in Paris at the end of the 19th century], slobbering mud and rubies, is the mouth of a tomb, buried church,
a subterranean temple (as in Egypt): the flickering muzzle of the
god-jackal Anubis, guide to the underworld. While, above, the
flame—inverted pubic-hair triangle—of the oil-lamp streetlight
rises from the wick which gathers as a storm, as a storm gathers, the insults which comprise it, and the flame still always
reaches upward, perversely, no matter how the lamp sways:
poetry of Baudelaire. Baudelaire. Not funeral wreaths dried in
cities without evenings could serve as offerings to him when the
very city's shimmering reality is the ghost, the soul, of Baude-

laire, like an atmospheric element we must breathe even if it kills us."

[What are "cities without evening" but reality in poetry?]

Paragraphs on pages do seem like clouds, like the interesting dirt behind the detergent container in the cupboard. And the men go somersaulting through them, physically fighting, suggesting sexual stories on the scale of cracked teacups.

Those who deliver the new poetry make it possible for the world to go on. Otherwise we would falter and harm ourselves as the repressed and neurotic do. (Though no one would even notice.) Because nothing is known that can't be expressed, and the existing, but unexpressed, is the source of buggy behavior. (Though no one would even notice.) [New poetry shows us God: how things are.]

The poets aren't supposed to be beautiful or sane. Shaggy, itchy, preoccupied, mal-educateds. It's a dirty and stressful and anti-social calling.

[Does consciousness really evolve?]

Cartoons as paradise. Wistful yearning for cartoons. Cartoons as eternity. Daffy Duck, Mickey Mouse, Bugs Bunny, Woody Wood-pecker, Roadrunner ... The Simpsons count too. The sparkle of Daffy's oily feathers in the eyes of Bart. Maniacally cackling amidst the mint-condition can of Rumford's Baking Powder, cel-luloid earring, Speedy Gonzales, the latest from Helen Topping Miller's fertile escritoire, a sheaf of suggestive pix on greige, deckle-edged stock ... Animated cartoons and comic books the pinnacle of the 20th century. Walt Disney's *Pinocchio*. Oh, I will diffuse exquisitely in a mist of brave surrender to desire for entrance into great cartoons. Can I not be rewarded for this? If I think of a sunset landscape panorama for Porky Pig beckoning to me on my deathbed, can't I get some points? Do I have a witness as I swing up over the horizon like a boy on a fishing expedition? I think I do. I believe I do. Love is its own reward too. The orchestra swells "ping boing wee wee" as cross-eyed satyrs whose furry ears are really more like bunnies' than goats' poop two-dimensional stars ...

Can you feel it? Or is it the worldly person's form of sentimentality? Are the cartoons really appealing because they're safe and have the proportions of children? But I love them, I love them so much.

Mallarmé was the Kurt Gödel of poetry ... Stable and self-contained systems [of description, of knowledge, of information] are always flawed, incomplete [to the understanding]. A thing can only be known in terms from outside its own system, and that thing (system), in turn, can only be known in the terms of another, etc., ad infinitum. Symbolism (Mallarmé's writing) is the presentation of phenomena in a way that's consistent with this realization. ("Either mathematics is too big for the human mind or the human mind is more than a machine." –Gödel) It strives to present the truest, most beautiful rendition by presenting everything in terms of other things. [It's the extreme acknowledgment of metaphor as the essence of poetry.] (Or "rational thought can never penetrate to the final ultimate truth." –R. Rucker, describing Gödel's Incompleteness Theorem) Poem as thing describing thing describing thing as poem. (Ouroboros.)

The gutter drain "slobbering mud and rubies"–that's not American, is it? You can tell right away. It sounds like a translation. My first guess would be Baudelaire, though in fact it is: Mallarmé (alluding to Baudelaire–it's a poem toward a monument for him). I remember how hard it was to enjoy such stilted-seeming, alien constructions [phraseologies], at first. Reading translations is hard. At the same time a case could be made that for the serious reader, poetry is best read in translation. All writing is just means. It has no existence (as writing–though it can have an existence as reflex, as compulsion) outside of the effects it produces in its readers. Reading a poem in translation forces one to grope for, to study, to intensely focus on extracting the full possibilities of it in a way less likely to be undertaken in relation to the (original) accessible language. It also forces one to surrender to the writer/text, to grant it the benefit of all doubt . . . In fact, in an interview in 1891, Mallarmé himself said, "I believe, to the contrary, that there must only be allusion. The contemplation of objects, the images that soar from the reveries they have induced, constitute the song. The *Parnassians*, who take the object in its entirety and show it, lack mystery; they take away from readers the delicious joy that arises when they believe that their own minds are creating. To *name* an object is to suppress three-quarters of the enjoyment of the poem, which derives from the pleasure of step-by-step discovery; to suggest, that is the dream. It is the perfect use of this mystery that constitutes the symbol: to evoke an object little by little, so as to bring to light a state of the soul or, inversely, to choose an object and bring out of it a state of the soul through a series of unravelings." What does a translation do but allude?

I see a magnificent panorama of intellectual and sensual activities flowering across the open skies like confetti or the internal organs of developed motion picture film. In the future, all poetry will be translation.

13

In a way it's like finding God—to discover you've come to prefer faces that are no longer young. I like adult faces now, the ones more pliant, porous, noses prominent; faces in which are set eyes that look outwards, seeing, rather than on which are set eyes which merely decorate; where vanity has moved from lying buried to becoming exposed to eroding and getting blown away. Of course, I'm middle-aged myself, so it could be said that I'm biased, but it's logical that to age is to approach God. God: the truth of death, reply to death, replacement for death.

The young are so obvious, so oblivious, so grossly undefined, while nevertheless confined to themselves, self-obsessed. The only natural virtue of the young is sensitivity, and usually it's misdirected. Even the sexiness of youth is over-vaunted. Their formlessness of character undermines one's pleasure in their highly defined bodies.

An older face is a pretty demonstration of a sin defeated, namely vanity, and an individual born, knowing of the world and conscious of mortality. When one does know the world, one doesn't care to pretend to be other than oneself, whatever one's weaknesses and failings—affectations drop away—because one comes to realize that one's mixture of traits is its own justification, is perfection.

This is not me, "Paul," writing, this is God (my author) revealing my thoughts and feelings, speaking them in spite of me, of my inarticulateness, my dumb brutishness, because I am His ...

Do I protest too much? No, I really mean it. "Let the dead bury the dead," and let the young fuck the young (but as for you, go and proclaim the kingdom of God). I love to see the face of a forty-year-old I'd like to fuck, imagining her succumbing to the erotic waves, her learnèd, considered appreciation of them, yielding to them, even perhaps a delicious slight autumnal feeling. The knowing. The sublime consciousness of it all ... And the dignity penetrated.

It's a relief to find evidence of one's own "maturity," to notice oneself becoming ruled less by biological impulses. And also a relief to see thereby that one's still changing! Age has its lessons and information; it's not just loss and sleepiness ...

What about those awful face-lifts? Badges of shortfall I'd say, of life in an unfortunate side-dimension. It hurts to look at them. Of course everyone wants to look good, but "good" doesn't mean "young." "Good" means self-possessed and understanding. If you can do that with a face-lift, you're a better man than me (which may well be) ...

But then, suppose there was a young person who was without vanity, who was unaffected and wise. Oh shit! I'm a big liar! You couldn't beat that. It's giving me the most wonderful hint of a hardon right now. I want to fuck her tits!

Carried along in this stratum of glittery rainbow whip, become it, isolated from all other phenomena for a sentence ...

Then again ... T. was young. (But so was I.)

I was just looking at the book of T.'s poems. It reminds me there was a kind of secret he had: that he didn't write his poems himself. I mean he didn't write them *as* himself. He imagined the author(s) of the poems. That was a big discovery for him (at the age of fifteen!). It was like human evolution: We separate from the other animals (separate from our childhood) in becoming self-conscious and realizing that we're going to die; then, literarily, T. advanced past that, past "human," to "self-choice" (or "self"-subversion) (future: genetic engineering, cloning, electronic immortality?). The writer of his poems was usually either a pure version of whatever mood or insight was possessing him or a fantasy of himself he was having, but sometimes he did imagine himself as (a highly word-savvy version of) someone he knew or'd met or seen, and sometimes he made the author up in his imagination, as a fiction. Also, he let language have its way with him. But the poems' sources weren't "characters" or anything like that—the poems were all "his"—it was just a writing technique. Anyway, he explained it to me one night after he'd taken some speed. He said people half-consciously choose who they are anyway, how to present themselves, so why not go all the way? It's all appearances, and what is art but playing with appearances, etc., etc. Finally, though, it was just his means for writing as well as he could. I think once he conceived it and practiced it for a little while he didn't think about it anymore. People's big ideas are usually just the keys to their own problems.

I may be in the loony bin but I am *not* an unreliable narrator. I'm acquainted with a lot of crazy people and I can tell you that once you've spent time with them, it's obvious which ones lie. They're so indiscriminate about it, and they'll contradict themselves. True, it can be chilling the first time you realize it. But then half the time it's endearing. Of course serial killers don't get sent up here. This isn't even a real loony bin—it's more like a holding pen, for quarantine and observation. They put you here when you seem risky or in trouble. I've never been here for more than a month.

Speaking of unreliable nuts, though, today something funny happened. There's this patient called Tamoo. (He's not anything ethnically exotic—he just named himself that.) He's a sweet, smiley kid in his early twenties—wire-rim glasses, shortish, skinny, dirty-blond—who's always drawing with a magic marker and giving the drawings away to people on the ward. He walks up to people—whatever they're doing—and cheerfully tells them about something that's happened to him recently and about a picture he drew which he then offers. He's been here almost a month and is due to be discharged soon. When you're in that long they start to give you privileges, like supervised smoking breaks out front and even a free half-hour to take a walk or go to a grocery. So he had a half-hour pass today but he didn't come back on time. An hour passed, an hour and a half. Serious violation, lots of bad vibes and static. Finally he shows up and it turns out that what happened was he decided he wanted a haircut so he went and got one at a barber-shop, but of course he didn't have any money. Ha ha! I wish I could have seen that. I hope the barber was nice though.

No, my delusions are different. I just get tired and can't hold myself together for people. I like Aubrey Beardsley and Walt Disney and Jeff Koons (sometimes). I guess I'm a sex freak. I love Baron Corvo. I want to take my pants off and squeeze the two halves of my buttocks with my two hands. Maybe I'll just stick my hands down the back of my pants.

T. loved innocent beings like Tamoo. But more to the point: like me. I know that's why he went with me. I was like his boyfriend Gabby Hayes or Walter Brennan, subserviant older wiseguy of a sidekick, heavy drinker, who in my case also wanted to suck his dick. I liked to be a clown for him, I liked to anticipate his wants, I liked to needle him.

Meditate on the knowledge that the rest of life is what follows that time.

14

T. got close to one of his crazy friend John Schwartz's friends, Catherine. John Schwartz knew her from the hospital. She was nineteen and had dropped out of Barnard. The doctors' diagnosis of her was that she was a paranoid schizophrenic. That was worth some helpful medicine, but the prescriptions and dosages were always shifting and her episodes were frequent. Sometimes she didn't take the medicine. She often sought out Terence when her mind started to go.

One early autumn day they decided to walk up to the Gotham Book Mart in midtown, about forty blocks—two miles—from the Lower East Side. The sharp air was like liquor, like crisp thick Aquavit from the freezer, or fermented rough cider.

Catherine was tall, almost as tall as T., and her hair was dark red-blond. She had deep-set eyes, high cheekbones, and sea-shell white skin that was palely freckled and nearly poreless, as smooth as water. She was big and pretty enough that when T. first met her his impression was of power and independence, but though she was proud and kept to herself, he quickly learned about her fragility. She was frank with him about it. That morning he saw uncertainty in her face but they didn't refer to it.

They were happy to be making the excursion they'd planned.

New York seemed dignified and demure and teeming with treasure in the hour just after noon when they started uptown. They walked up Second Avenue a few blocks and shifted west through the little park that faced the Quaker meeting house above 15th Street. The air was windy. They looked at the buildings and talked about what the streets and weather made them think of.

Broad, bland Third Avenue with its small apartment buildings over ephemeral bar-restaurants wasn't very tempting and neither were the camera shops and delis and tall office buildings of Park. They walked further west and then turned right to take Broadway's diagonal up past the Flatiron Building and across Fifth and Sixth Avenues via the street's intelligent and actually narrow path of vintage New York business districts, toward Times Square, where they had the idea of getting lunch.

"Man, New York does make me happy," said T.

"Yeah," said Catherine, wild-eyed.

As they walked he let his hand brush hers and it was like walking on the moon. They'd had sex a couple of times, and Catherine had seemed frantic for it, but T.'d wondered whether her abandon came not so much because she cared for him and felt safe but because she was fleeing her brain. Then, at another time, she'd seemed to do it by decision and he'd wondered whether the sex might be a courtesy she showed him. She knew about Paul.

Looking at her made his own reality more delicate, not because she was crazy, but because he liked her so much.

They stopped to sit under the trees just above 23rd Street in Madison Square Park for a minute.

"I've been having problems," she said.

"You have?"

"Yeah." The rims of her eyes were red. "I am a problem child."

94

"What's happened?"

"The usual."

"Is it bad?"

"I don't know, not really."

"What happens?"

"Well," she began, "windows want me to jump out of them." But she still seemed as if she could start crying.

"Oh . . ."

"Why are they there if you're not supposed to go through them?"

"They're there so there's light and space instead of just blank walls."

"It doesn't make any sense . . . What do you know? You were brought up in a cave."

"Yeah I was raised by goats."

"So what do you know?"

"Nothing."

He stood up and did some kind of weird jig, his head bent forward and index fingers pointing up along his temples. Ridiculous as he looked, it was also grotesque enough that she might have actually been shocked. You could see that in her face. She laughed though.

They started back up Broadway. After a block T. took her hand. He smiled inwardly at his juvenile imagination. He held her hand as if it was natural, but the linking of their hands charged them so that it was like they became invisible; they could see everything with more knowledge than the things they were looking at. Catherine seemed calmed and happy. They looked in the store windows and watched the people that passed.

They arrived at Times Square and looked for where to get lunch. Times Square was battered and scratched but cozy, with the theater marquees lining 42nd Street advertising genre movies and exploitation movies and second-run double features, the sidewalks dark with furtive people looking for trouble, and trouble advertising itself somewhat furtively from the midst of jumbo timeless-seeming neon signs, novelty shops, and games parlors. They found a tiny lucheonette tucked among the dusty tourist traps along Seventh Avenue near 47th Street and took a two-person table along the wall. They opened up the sharp-edged laminated menus a guy handed them across the counter and read the listings and looked at the shiny though faded-looking color pictures of three or four of the place's most appetizing entrees.

T. saw her get stalled as she read. She was frowning at the plaque of a menu, her face uncertain and almost ashamed. T. looked back at his and in a minute saw that the big picture of spaghetti with meatballs was captioned "Fried Chicken Dinner." He asked, "Can I look?" and reached across and pulled her menu around and it was the same. She smiled but with an embarrassed look.

T. laughed happily, not quite fully aware. He asked: "Have you been out in the sun? You look freckly."

"You sound freckly."

"No, really, you could almost be someone else, the way your face is like switched on so the ... freckles are highlighted."

"I *am* someone else. I don't like my freckles, don't you know that? You said I was like a female cardinal. Why did you say that?"

"Because I like female cardinals."

"I see through you, bird-boy ... Don't get me wrong." She looked really frightened and ashamed.

They ate a little bit. In a minute he caught her looking at him in a startled way and she said, "Where's your arm?"

"This is my arm."

96

"I want to go," she said. "Can we go someplace quieter?"

"How about Central Park, or Bryant Park?"

"OK."

They went outside. She said, "Everything dead is alive. Everything alive is dead."

"Let's go to Bryant Park—it's closer. Or do you want to get a cab home?"

"I'm dreaming," she said. T. pulled her through the doorway of a building and into a corner of the little vestibule in front of revolving doors. She looked at him distraught but insistently.

"What do you want to do?" he asked. "Where do you want to go? Can you think of a good place?" She looked close to panic. "Do you want to get a drink?"

"Yes."

"We need a liquor store because I don't know any place they're going to serve me around here."

The drinking softened things, and they drank for the next few hours. They eventually passed out, and when T. woke up he found her writing his name in her lower belly with a razor blade, and he talked her into checking into the hospital.

There were features typical of her episodes: the inanimate becoming animate (chairs being insects) and the animate inanimate (people mechanical: "Where's your arm?! That's not really your arm!"); and her sense that the world was being revealed as it actually is, only free of the distortions and interpretations imposed by the brain, without hierarchies or classifications or stories, and, most importantly and frighteningly, without the world having any relation to her. It was a kind of spectacular hell, with no emotion except for the sadness and panic that followed from her memory that it hadn't always been that way, that there was a more comforting state that she'd known.

When she was OK, T. would try to talk about it with her, hoping it might help. "You know I think you actually are seeing things the way they are, or in a way that is more correct than the ordinary ways of seeing things, but if it's agonizing and horrifying there's something wrong with it. That's all there is to it. Truth is harmony if you're going to be alive. It may be a highly customized kind of harmony, but it's harmony. Suffering is only right as a means to an end. I wish that instead of arguing with me you'd try to see it this way. You are not apart from things."

He told Paul that one loves the person who gives oneself expression by being receptive, by being capable of perceiving oneself. Most of the time we are only a little alive, like a book in an obscure language. But because of those who can read us, who understand us and what we are signifying, we are brought to life, and we love them for realizing us.

15

One summer night, six or seven months after T.'d arrived in town, he stood on a tabletop in the noisy little dark back room of Max's Kansas City and pissed into a champagne glass, and Paul took a sip before throwing it in Sam Pryor's face. A brawl ensued. They broke a Dan Flavin fluorescent light bulb. A platinum-blond waitress slipped on dried chick peas awry and busted her nose. T. and Paul were permanently eighty-sixed.

They weren't welcome among the artists anywhere anymore. As poets, they socialized only with each other and, now and then, Ted, drinking, and when they went out it was to the cheapest lushes' bars, where Paul was known and his sixteen-year-old companion had no problem being served. The legal drinking age was only eighteen but T. did look young. T. was a glaring, articulate, angry drinker, Paul a silly, dramatic, sentimental one, but they both drank to become unpredictable.

T. would get menial "grey-market" jobs—lugging cement bags around a nonunion construction site, filing folders in an office for a temp agency, delivering packages—which he'd quit as soon as he had enough money to live for another few weeks. Paul had the civil service desk job his father-in-law had gotten him, but he showed up as little as he could get away with.

They spent the greatest amount of their time together reading and writing and sometimes talking in T.'s apartment. These were probably their best times too despite being experienced largely as tedium. They preferred the times of thrills, but the thrills grew out of the tension; and the mild, mildly restless, half-frustrated times of the many nights and late afternoons of doing almost nothing in T.'s apartment, or walking the streets without direction, were their true lives.

T.'s room was like some kind of glum office in its lack of daylight and its featurelessness, but with the little pictures now tacked on the walls, and the typewriter and sheets of paper, and the drugs, it got some character. He'd picked up a few stray pieces of furniture on the streets, including a table and three chairs, crates for shelves, and a beat-up old oriental rug. There was a secondhand portable record player too and a few albums.

They drank coffee and beer and sometimes codeine cough syrup and sometimes smoked some grass or snorted a little THC or mescaline and every once in a while a tiny bit of heroin, but mostly they lay around and lazily, impatiently goofed and wrote and complained, goading each other. Sometimes in the middle of the night one of them would go out for a container of fresh ice cream from Gem's Spa. They'd go to a movie sometimes, or wander the rows of used bookstores on Fourth Avenue, or drink in a bar, but most of the time was spent in the dim back apartment.

The days and nights were as endless as wallpaper patterns. Boredom and irritation were normal and lengthened out into sometimes-mean giggles and into pages of writing. Writing was their pay. Books were reality. The room was a cruder dimension-poor annex to the pages of writing. The writing, as casual as it was—smeared eraseable typing-pages with revisions scribbled on and crumpled pages of rejected tries—was the brightly lit and wildly littered universe erupting out from the dark, poor, inexpressive room.

How odd is it to have as a purpose in life the aim of treating life—in the medium created for the purpose of coldly corresponding to it, words—as raw material for amusing variations on itself? Sometimes T. and Paul fantasized about this, imagining themselves as godlike philosopher poets encouched in the advanced civilization, languorously sipping their fermented grain as they spun ideas and mental-sensual constructions of life-language in the air for the pleasure of their own delectation.

Paul sat on the futon inside the apartment door, his back against the wall beside it, looking to his left, out the adjoining wall's near window framing leaves and branches and the brick back wall of the tenement on the next street. T. was sunk in a threadbare dingy armchair seated perpendicular to Paul's stretched body across the small room and directed more or less toward the other back window. His feet were up on a fruit crate and his head was lowered toward the small hardcover book he was reading.

> There is a dog outside made of birds.
> There's a cathedral coming down and a lake going up.
> There's no recognition between two beings that see each
>   other.
> There's a festival in the dark held by forms of blindness.

There's a roll of toilet paper on the bare floor beside T.'s chair because he blows his nose a lot.

"Snot is white blood cells that've died fighting germs."

"Noble fluid."

Later T. stands up and moves toward the kitchen deliberately slowly like a two-dimensional, hinged paper puppet of an old man, or a clumsy imitation of one. Paul watches this. In the kitchen T. calls out, "Beer?" He pours two glasses and returns with them in the same exaggerated cartoon style.

After following him with his eyes for a moment, Paul stopped looking. What was T. doing? Was it a form of communication, saying, "Even though we haven't talked now for an interval, I'm acknowledging that you're here" (in the same way a person might hum during a silence where he wouldn't if he was alone) "while mocking myself too, all in a friendly gesture to you." Or was it a comment on the unreality of everything and a sign of alienation? Or was it an attempt to disrupt? Or was it an expression of passing discomfort? Or was he just being childish, silly? It was uncertain. Did it happen at all? Was that the question?

You can feel boredom inside you, as if everything inside your skin has turned to a kind of dry nougat of fossilized sleep, stale sleep. It also has an effect on your salivary glands: They work a little harder and secrete a thinner product. This boredom is always mixed with particles of frustration and anger.

But beer dispels it, though it can hurt your stomach and make you grouchy as you become sedated, sleep badly, and wake up.

Paul said, "Let's write something."

"OK," said T., "you start," as he continued to read the little book which he grasped skeptically in his long hands like something that could possibly come alive and need to be flung away.

Paul walked over and hefted the little lightweight grey Olivetti portable that sat on some telephone books in the corner behind T. and brought it back with a few sheets of paper to his place against the wall. He rolled in a piece of crisp "Corrosible Bond" and looked at it.

The typing made a snapping sound. "Spatial grain descended as flesh internal [. . .]" He looked at that and then put a hyphen between "flesh and "internal" and then added a second line, "tints; the light was tired and canine."

He stood and brought the typewriter over to T. and returned to the futon where he took a drink of beer and lay on his back, his head on a pillow at the base of the wall. He lit a cigarette.

T. looked at the typewriter in his lap. He looked at it for a while, and then added a new line, "Bluebells dimly strove to serve," and then he pushed the carriage back and on the next line typed, "as the pallbearers of exhausted virginity."

"All right," T. said, and laboriously balanced the typewriter on the arm of the chair, lifted himself up, and carried the machine back over to Paul.

Paul looked at the paper on the platen, smiled half-forcedly, and then grunted, "Huhn." He smoked his cigarette and looked at the page and scratched his eye. He stretched and yawned and thought and looked at the paper. T. was back in his chair, now a little more lively and alert, peering at his book, drinking his beer. He lit a cigarette too. It was nice how quiet it was in the back apartment even though the bottom half of the window on T.'s side was wide open.

T.'d put a few things on the walls. There was a collage by John Schwartz. It featured a black-and-white pornography-magazine photo of the rear view of a naked woman standing outside, apparently by a swimming pool, among tall, leafy trees. The one-fourth view of her face showed her to be pretty and sporting a carefree smile. She had an elaborate, chic-looking hairdo and wore a two-strand pearl necklace with matching earrings. The picture was burned around its edges and pasted to a sheet of lined composition-book paper on which, below the image, was ballpoint-inked in bulbous script the words, "These maple leaves are so good to reminisce over!"

There was a color print from a Fourth Avenue bookshop of a pair of barn swallows with that typical old-fashioned ornithological artist's exaggeration of the swooping lines of the birds. They were caught against a soft white-blue sky delineating their creamy gold and cinammon breasts, long narrow wings triumphantly upraised, the crisp feathers of their forked tails as pretty as the flourish of an artist's illegible signature, rust-colored masks in the blue-black hoods of their blue-black capes, the longer-tailed bird dangling an insect into the beak of the other.

There was a photobooth picture strip of T. with a shy, ethereal, smiling Catherine.

There was a publicity headshot of Priscilla Lane.

Paul typed a new line: "Yes, all phenomena not associated with the human"—carriage return, line break—"leant to serve. We were happy […]"

He gave the typewriter back to Randall, who wrote:

> or at least we thought we were. In
> retrospect perhaps we were something else, something
> less human, as inhuman as conceivable.

He looked at what he'd typed, and then added:

> Around the corner careened a car
> alive with slaves to psycho-pop.

Paul put:

In the ruins I lie thinking of you in
patterns of weeping tic tac toe graphics.

T. took out the period at the end of that line and wrote below it:

and turn, and turning turn and turning turn
ing turn until like Turing I'm a bird on
a bicycle suicided by turds.

When Paul saw that he frowned. "Can I take out 'turds'—I don't
think this poem should have turds in it."

"Reconsider."

Paul said slowly, "Now that I've reconsidered I see that you're
correct."

"You can take it out if you have to, but you better write something better … If it rhymes with 'birds' it can't be all bad … Doesn't
it seem like there are certain-sounding words that get to be the
bad words? Like 'uck': fuck, muck, duck, suck, guck, etc. But then
there's 'luck' too. 'Urd': nerd, curd, turd, murder. But then you do
have 'word' and 'bird.'"

Spatial grain descended as flesh-internal
tints; the light was tired and canine.
Bluebells dimly strove to serve
as the pallbearers of exhausted virginity.
Yes, all phenomena not associated with the human
leant to serve. We were happy
or at least we thought we were. In
retrospect perhaps we were something else, something
less human, as inhuman as conceivable.

Around the corner careened a car
alive with slaves to psycho-pop.
In the ruins I lie thinking of you in
patterns of weeping tic tac toe graphics
and turn, and turning turn and turning turn
ing turn until like Turing I'm a bird on
a bicycle suicided by turds.

"Not one of our finer efforts," said Paul. "It's a little 'John Ashbery.'"

Later T. let Paul mess with his undressed body. The sex they had
was so exciting to Paul that he felt like he had to try and restrain
himself because it could put T. off.

Near midnight the following evening, T. still had not slept. Paul
was passed out on the futon. T. stood with a knife and an apple at
the counter in the kitchen. There were tears on his face. Somehow
he'd started crying about coring an apple.

***

I wouldn't be surprised if I were to find myself back in that room
as I faded. Maybe that premonition of dying as "subsiding back" is
literally true. Maybe that's what people mean by their whole lives
passing before them as they die. Maybe you slip back through the
things that formed you and I actually will return to that room.

But once something is over, it's not real anymore, is it? All there is
is the present, and the past is just a shading or even fantasy influence.

I guess I'm not a very good believer–Catholic. I love Jesus but at
the same time I know I can only approach my imagination of Him.

106

16

Past life really is a text, a work, a novel. The things you think
happened aren't any more true than a book. Lives differ as
much in their complexity as books or movies. Books and
movies are better though because their characters don't have feelings. So let's fly, my darlings, into the leaning heights of folded
linen.

It's all smudged and smeared. Those bony boy's buttocks of his,
I didn't have much to compare them to; to me they were the rear
view of his hardon, or what his cock was hidden by, or the way to
his cock. I haven't seen too many men's behinds and I never had
that gay thing about boys' butts really (while I do like women's)…
Meanwhile, an Other's perception of the "same" events is so
unlike one's own. Yes, we do operate in these scarcely overlapping
fields, calling to each other from great distances, colors and sounds
and smells and tastes incommunicable. Butting up against each
other: Only touch, touch which is to stimulate the sense receptors
of another with one's own same class of sense receptors. Though
this is true also in a limited way of the senses of taste and smell,
which perhaps is why to kiss is the most intimate: tongue tasting
tongue, nose smelling nose, face feeling face. Prostitutes often don't

allow kissing. To kiss is to share the world most completely.

It's funny to be living in an imaginary place, but I love the past of blaze and haze. We know that there's a sense in which everything's brilliant and I'll pretend to it.

***

One weekend that winter Paul and T. passed a car on the street with a "For Sale" sign on it. It was a little 1965 Barracuda, dark green, for $600. T. told Paul he should buy it.

That night they were drinking in a dive on Third Avenue near 13th Street and T. brought it up again, and you could almost see on his face what his mind was doing. He was realizing he could leave New York the way he'd left Covington, Kentucky, and he liked the idea and was already becoming fixed on it. It was scary to Paul, but T. wanted him to be part of it, so it became scary in an exciting way.

T. said, "We don't need to be here. These people are idiots."

"New York ain't only people."

"I know. It's movies too and all-night delis, blah blah blah, but you can't see the night sky here, and everybody is an asshole and they're just holding us back. The world we were made to know smells better. Plus it's time for a new adventure."

"What about my wife and Alex?"

"She doesn't even know you and she bores you and there's nothing you can do about the baby. Let's get out of here. Let's go to Texas or Mexico. We could live at the shore of the ocean where there are also deserts and mountains. Think of it."

"What are we supposed to do for money?"

"This country is rich and we're smart. There's money everywhere. We could become tycoons if we're not careful. Money is easy."

"Come on."

"Paul, you have money. Take the nine hundred dollars. Your wife's parents are rich. She'll be fine. The important thing is for us to snap out of it."

"Speak for yourself."

"We have to snap out of it. Nine hundred dollars'll go a lot further in Texas too."

"What's this with 'Texas?'"

"Well, it's close to Mexico and it has a shore. Sure, it's rednecks but I couldn't take California. Or Florida. Actually North Florida might not be bad. Maybe we should try Florida first. It's probably safer and there's all that free fruit and plenty of seafood. We could go by Memphis on the way. I've always wanted to see Memphis. Man, think of it. We could get away from all these fake writers."

Paul piped, "All right, let's do it . . . Florida. But we should take a bus or a train. The car costs too much. We're going to need all the money we can get."

"All right Paul!"

17

Bus rides were beautiful in those days, or maybe it's that they become the youthful.

Paul and T. left two days later! They got tickets to Memphis even though it was way out of the way, further west than they needed to go.

Stepping into the bus was like walking into a soft cloth-upholstered opium den for the excited poets: from the curbside underground at Port Authority Bus Terminal up three steps into the close space, big dark scuffed windows, and deeply-stuffed but springy seats. A smell like wet straw. They had everything they were bringing in two small cases. T. sat at a window on the right side of the grey metal vehicle a little past halfway back and Paul sat next to him. It was late February and the window was cold.

"The positive anonymity of leaving is preferable to the negative anonymity of loving," said T., thinking aloud.

Sound was muffled in the bus and people seemed to whisper from respect.

T. felt that leaving New York signified something more. He felt a kind of regret for he didn't know what, an anxiety at unknowable results, as at the necessity of an instant choice, like in a falling airplane. But the performance of the act was exhilarating. It was mythology, a choice of one door from among three. It was metaphysical, and there was something about it that felt adult in a way that he hadn't quite felt before. Maybe that was what was new. He had a passing twinge of feeling that Paul was superfluous, which seemed cruel in a way that he didn't like, and he was surprised that he didn't like it, which was also surprising itself.

Paul felt ignited, transgressing.

Outside, the driver lowered the hatch over the luggage-stow and latched it. He climbed onto the bus, dropped down into his seat, pulled the door-lever, checked the mirrors, shifted into gear, released the air-brakes, and backed out of the parking slot. He turned the bus the long spiral up to the streets and onto the feed-ramp into the Lincoln Tunnel. T. felt like he was on a conveyor belt and it was out of his hands and it was fine.

They had some pills and some whiskey. The bus, giant capsule, was about three-quarters full. There was a woman with an infant child in the pair of seats directly behind Paul and T. The baby seemed like chaos and the smush-faced pee of her mother.

The poets got giddy. There was snow on the ground once they got outside of New York City. The baby in the seats behind would cry, begging to be dealt with. The whiskey alone was sufficient riches. Paul and T. sang together in semi-whispers and groped each other in the bus-ride novelty. It was like eloping.

T. had bought a bunch of underground comic books for reading matter. He loved those, he really loved Robert Crumb.

It was interesting to inventory the phenomenal input.

They had bags of peanuts and bars of chocolate too, and their scuffed notebooks.

Within a couple of hours Paul had passed out.

T. felt a suffusing pleasure for having subsided into this new crowd of unknown people. It was like being reborn to be one of the number defined by the capacity of the bus. He was no one no one no one. He was confused and full of errors like everybody on the bus. People could only understand him on their own terms and the same was true of him regarding them. He had to reconsider what his purpose was.

T. remembered he'd brought along a new poem of Ted's.

> The skywriting of all things was
> directed at me, leering "Come at once
> or the plums may rot!" Well,
> naturally I thought I should comply, so
>
> I plumped my lobes, bid adieu
> to everyone I ever knew (but you–which's
> why I'm writing now of course),
> adjusted foreskin, knocked one back, and
>
> fled to that small town. Having thought better.
> But there the falling leaves proved hung
> on sturdy limbs! That hurt! And I
> felt badly disassociated.
>
> Then another biplane happened over!
> How could it be? A parachutist bended
> towards me, took my hand, and guided it. Oh
> relief! So it was all precisely as intended!

Oh my god. It's about the trip before Ted even knew! It was funny and kind of pretty but it felt frustrating. Words of poetry, of some kind of exhibitionist wisdom. They were false comfort, egotism, distraction, weren't they? T.'s brain hurt. He itched. He was angry at himself. The poems were pointless, an obstacle, warped keyhole, just more data, more code to interpret, laid over, or added to all the existing. Someone stamping things with personality and point of view. Making everything human for the humans. It was fine, it was normal, but it was sad and wrong. What about the poetry from other planets? He felt angry and he worried that he was going crazy, that everything was wasted. Why couldn't he settle into life? He felt nauseous, horrified.

You write things down to keep them. Or to assert: *This* is interesting.

It was just coming to be dawn outside. T. gave himself to the dawn, dreamed in the dawn, dreamed its bidding.

18

Groups of travelling strangers are pockets of roiling sex, like the end of the world, desert island. Everybody falls in love on boats and trains and buses. Using the toilet is a bore but at least the bus wasn't too full. Sleeping hurt the neck. The bus's progress did seem slow even after only one night. It was about a twenty-hour drive (Jersey, PA, West Virginia, Ohio, KY, Tennessee). Cheeto crumbs, candy wrappers.

T. felt a kind of rigid loneliness. He felt like a ship's figurehead or a hood ornament. Garbo's Queen Christina. Advancing sharply through the surroundings, continuously leaving everything behind. He smiled at the dramatics, but it did feel powerful to be unleashed again.

He felt as if his story was creating its own logic. That because he'd left New York, where a purpose had taken him, that his purpose must be different now too. That he was who he was because of what he did, rather than the other way around; he didn't want an "inner life." And that he was watching his minor destiny as it played out.

His mind groped for poetry. It was a weakness.

Maybe his identity was in leaving. That would be funny. The

bus away sure felt sexy.

He reclined and lay back in his seat as far as possible and closed his eyes and felt his mind drawn halt in snatches toward a certain view, an effort, a kind of mental feat of reaching, semi-accomplished, like trying to solve a hard mathematical problem without paper, like trying to gather grain in an armful: The aim was to be aware of everything in the world at once, everything human anyway, which was also all time since all time still existed–the social stages: tribal hunters, cities of warlords, post-industrial republics; and all experience as well: hunger, sleep, awe, contempt, murder, discovery, kindness, doubt . . . It wasn't possible to really hold it in mind–it would be like having a perfect memory–but it was amusing to try to skirt and press and contemplate. One's own location, immediate environment, was infinitesimal but there were threads to everything. It was an antidote to false ambition. It created a healthy ennui. It was nauseating.

And then there was one's imagination . . .

He thought of movies. He thought of himself thinking. It was as boring as literature! What on earth was there to do?

He shuddered.

And then you open your eyes and phenomena make your twisting mind a joke.

He thought of his father who'd left the family before T. knew him. His mother cursed him (in her proper way), but T. could understand he had to have the freedom and adventure.

He wrote in his notebook.

> Bus crunches through the
> Perpendicular shutters to the road.
> The hands of hula
> Dancers dart between the rods and cones.

Teeth crunch recollected
Flowers recollected
And the legendary lady
In the front row farts. I

Adore her, adore her
I loosely, so
As to into
Tears collapse on the one

Hand, while on the other
Chocolate
Figures in colored foil
Come to life and speak.

They say, "Welcome
Bugs swarm on it,
Girls are half made,
A heron overhead drops

Straight down to crash
At his feet. "Is this the
World," it asks. There
Is no such thing to the living.

The baby in the seat behind was jabbering. Paul woke up. T. twisted around and looked back over the top of his seat and said, "Grow up." Paul laughed and closed his eyes again.

***

Everything is true but nothing is permitted–this would be a good title for an article on Robert Bresson, my hero. Or even Borges. Whatever you can imagine exists, but you can only do what you're made to by the forces that drive things. Wow, I've shaded back into myself in the hospital.

Sometimes I think I'm his clone. That he planted genetic material that grew into me. I have ideas that aren't mine, they're his (convenient for an author!). For instance, the sense that I'm a node of "human being." That a "human being" is really everyone alive, and each "individual" is a cell of it, that consciousness itself is the entity, not individual people: It's everybody's awareness combined at once that is the being. Creepy, really.

***

Memphis was spooky with its wagon-era brick-paved streets, abandoned buildings, and ignored giant river that was both the center and the edge of town. The motel, The Motorman, where they stayed, bordered the matrix of downtown at a big intersection. At night the traffic in the parking lot was like a drive-in. Strangers would knock on their door, wanting to buy something or borrow something or say "hidey." The doorway was actually burnt. It was charred and black all along the length of its opening, as if at some time one of those visitors had gotten too excited to be denied.

The orange and brown patterns of the rough synthetic fabrics of the curtains and bedspread and carpet were probably intended to hide dirt, but things had gone beyond that. The bathtub was stained down its insides in ragged striae of brown and greenish-yellow, like a geological cross section, and the towels were not just threadbare but smelled rancid. The cloth throughout the rooms seemed moist, but in infinitesimal beads, as if it was meant to have rotted long ago but couldn't because it was a modern miracle synthetic: some kind of textile tale of Poe. The heavy carpet had mysterious stiff patches.

Paul kept thinking he could smell the burnt door, though he really couldn't. The odor of the room was like vaporized headache.

The whole city was depressing. People were suspicious of them. They had to run once from high school boys screaming, "Yankee shitheads! New York homos!" and chasing them in broad daylight for three blocks along a major thoroughfare.

T. would come back to the motel angry. The pair of them were worried about money. Paul felt inferior and exposed.

Elvis Presley lived a few blocks away. Beale Street was a dead-city low block of pawnshops and boarded-up windows, though it did still conceal a few old blues players from the plantations if you walked down the right stairs. In another part of town, Stax Records, in a converted movie theater, had a marquee out front and a Rolls Royce in its parking lot (for the time being). The tiny Sun Records one-story storefront was down a wide contrary. The city did seem like a place the justification of which was jumpy music. The playing came from dirt and returned to dirt, like people in bed and drunk and saying they were sorry to the "Lord" while they fucked at the wrong times and bled on everything.

T. was listening to that music. He already wanted to take an axe to the room, which was the devil's-abode part of the whole thing. He couldn't joke about the room, it was too much like a coffin built of woven fart in your head. The room had dibs on the mockery. The ape looked out from behind the clown. He kept drinking malted milk. Malted milk kept rushing to his head. His doorknob kept turning. It must have been spooks. The hair rising on his head: a warm old feeling.

Paul got more and more worried and he drank more and more. The college was playing Orson Welles movies and that was the best part for him.

There was a young black girl, very dark, with straightened bone-colored dyed hair, around the motel who would wink and whisper at the poets, mouthing phantom kisses and swinging her behind. She was skinny but had a noble chest, not large but hard-looking and upturned, as if it were strapped close like she was masquerading as a boy, and she flaunted the biggest sculpted high-set ass T. had ever seen. It was something T. wanted to see naked desperately and that could obviously be arranged.

Butt Becomes But

They brought her to the room and her crotch stank so they washed it off and out but she was alternately flirtatious and whiny and seemed mentally defective, so even though they jerked off on her it all seemed fucked up. Price: $30 for the pair of them.

T. asked her about his theory that you could predict the relative size of the penises of a racial group by the size of the women's asses—Africans big, Asians small, for instance—and she didn't seem to understand and got resentful and sulked but—as if accidentally—showed off her nipples.

She seemed to unprotestingly understand herself as being the property of others, but if her owners departed from established patterns of use she dulled out or got angry and intercourse was rerouted back to within the parameters, or else violence occurred. She expected her clients to be puffed up by owning her and they were, but it was so sad and infuriating that the ownership wasn't simple that it made them want to get back at her. She was fine with letting them gorge on her tits and spit on her and lick it off and have her lift her legs behind her neck and then probe with their cockheads curiously past the lips of her asshole. She didn't think badly of them but they might as well have been retarded children. The poet clients felt dirty and degraded and then it was over and they were alone again. They felt prostituted.

The Welles movies gave it all a tone for Paul too, as if he was in a delirium that made the movies as real as Memphis. They were an escape from his poverty, but they also invaded it, expanding it wider and deeper with more emptiness of cross-connected tunnels and jungle paths in the southern daylight. "It's a bright guilty world." The Welles movies themselves were crippled like Everett Sloane repeatedly drinking himself into a stupor. They were truncated and mutilated by the ways of the world. Still, the filmmaker managed to turn insipid Tim Holt into a tragic hero. Anne Bancroft was everything Paul'd ever wanted. Paul felt so lonely. "We live as we dream—alone." Welles was into Conrad; *Heart of Darkness* had been his choice for a film subject before *Citizen Kane*.

The poetry got somewhat bitter and angry and drunkenly erotic. Restraints were even fewer. And somehow in it they both found how kind-hearted they were. But the kind-heartedness itself was sad, like a loss of ideals, or a loss of faith in each other. Married life was hell.

T. would walk over to the Highland Strip, a block of street near the college where kids played pinball and pool and listened to music and tried to have sex and sold each other drugs and ate hamburgers. He was able to find out about a less sleazy motel and they moved.

Paul was drinking a whole lot. One night, about a week after they'd arrived in Memphis, T. came back to the motel room and found Paul on the phone with his wife. He mocked him.

Paul said to T., "I understand you." T. just shrugged his shoulders.

T. celebrated the stuck grains of shit in the hair of his ass. He dragged himself like his own farm animal through abandoned forgotten unseen streets where there was shit in the gutters and the poor people were like cattle and he was an angel among them, vomiting, with tears in his eyes.

We must follow his example or kill ourselves or die forgotten, not even regretted but just forgotten by all time like mush, like food that nobody wants unless they're starving and no one ever wants to remember again.

He said to Paul, the poets are despicable! They are worse than tyrants because they are deceivers and scum. They not only leave all life out of their poetry, but, whereas by writing a poem they affirm the value of poetry among all things, in their behavior they are as small and greedy and timid and cheap as the worst cowardly submitters to policemen and grovelers before public opinion.

But then the next moment he would say it's all a joke!

He was Satan!

His filthy humor came from clearly seeing the guts of things that everyone denied, his filthy humor came from science.

I was just a stupid wife whom he tolerated for company and out of charity.

While I'd thought we were two happy children free to wander in a Paradise of sadness.

***

I'm drunk!

Maybe only the writing was real! These stupid lives of ours.

But the thing about him, his grandeur, his Godliness, that can never be grasped by narrative nor analysis, was his ability to include all in a few lines. His gorgeous castles in the air were tethered by thick bloody ropes of guts (in the dawn). It was only words. No one is greater than another. But still I want to cry. What is the meaning of his failure, of his horrible life? Jesus failed! I'm sorry.

All poetry is translation! You must write your own poetry! Really, poetry must be written by all!

***

He had written a sonnet when he was fourteen:

Evening Prayer

I, an angel at toilet, sit
forever with beer, and smoking tobacco
and drinking my beers my head full of shit
(*dreams*) and I'm wacko

my head full of dreams that burn like phosphorous
heart like a hunk of raw torn wood
my head unwilling to act as the boss for us:
sad heart crying its gold sap blood

and once I've carefully swallowed the dreams
I turn from the beer and leave the room
to meadows outside where the burning deems

me Lord and I sweetly piss in the womb
of the dark skies high in glorious streams
that bless and gratify every bloom

19

The world turns and we become sick. He defined vertigos. I do believe that true life is elsewhere. We are not in the world. The things we do, their incoherence, their blindness and stupidity, are, in heaven, numberless pure friezes of glory. His poems are earthly frames and fragments, gauzes and gazes, of those golden eternities full of shit.

Life has a subtext. Isn't that an exciting idea?

The wonderful thing about poetry is that it really is always out of fashion. Poetry is the place of no low values. Poetry has no ambition but itself. That is how it refreshes, nourishes. "Poetry is making a comeback." But why is it always bad poetry, or a false idea of poetry, that is making a comeback? I don't think good poetry has ever made a comeback, or ever will. That's one reason it's necessary to keep on writing it. When I open a book to find a poem, I feel like I've gotten to heaven, where it's obvious what matters, while elsewhere what matters is hidden. It's joy. Or not. It's penetrating the veil as a matter of course.

It's interesting to grow older and see the ways in which people change. It seems there's a general pattern: free-wheeling self-certainty in early youth, followed by some bewilderment and reassessment after coming to a few dead ends, and then, if one has survived the reorganization, a middle age into which one's shape and dimensions more or less cleanly fit. The feeling of achievement in having learned what to expect and how to handle what arises and what one's true talents and qualities are is a great reward.

A little lithium and I'm a goddamn solid citizen.

But who will be interested in my theories? No one. Well, here are things he did. He lost interest in me. We all know what that's like. It makes your skin crawl. Nowadays they say "crawl" for the written messages scrolling across a surface like the bottom of the TV screen on a CNN report. Babies crawl before they can walk. Temple Grandin gets down on her hands and knees to know how a cow in a slaughterhouse feels shuttled through the chutes and passages toward death. But when skin crawls, one nearly vomits in a hidden dimension while frowning a little until drunk enough to maneuver in the wet cotton. Then, soon enough, eventually, one regains one's equilibrium. Such incompatibilities finally are their own consoling explanations: To be unable to tolerate one, the other can never be sad because all is as it must be. Love cannot be willed—quite the contrary—and once one knows what is, what is is locked (he taught me).

Once one knows what is, it is locked (he taught me). That's where quantum physics (in which the location of something or another is truly indefinite—not merely unknown—until one looks, at which time it becomes established), as "counterintuitive" as it is, is reflected in full scale, macro, human life. There is no disentangling the mind from the world. Look at Othello. Look at

Brigette Bardot (*Contempt*). "Thou shalt not bear false witness against thy neighbor." Because saying something creates it. (That's "magic." Plant an idea about someone and even once it's known for certain that it's untrue, it will continue to influence the perception of the person. It's a kind of magic curse that works in even the least superstitious society.) God said the world. In the beginning was the Word. Later, the Word was made flesh, and dwelt among us (and we beheld His glory, the glory as of the only begotten of the Father), full of grace and truth. (And T. did love science, but he also preached the error of taking an instance of scientific knowledge for a "philosophical" metaphor that was anything more than plastic and a fragile convenience, because even the most well-established of physical laws are subject to revision and have limiting contexts.) He loved learning, he loved studying, he loved libraries.

But how the skin crawls on being not loved. And to want love inhibits its generation! They say the skin is an organ, the body's heaviest. It's an organ that shivers in expression of certain emotions. Shuddering happens below the skin, goosebumps on its surface. But when the skin crawls it's a current conducted by the skin, and one feels queasy. The skin ripples, it moves against itself like cartoon worms, contracting and extending, or its layers slide in opposed directions back and forth like hands warming, and one is helpless, vertiginous, subjected to involuntary physical responses. So feelings do have immediate physical consequences. One isn't loved and the skin crawls and all the wrong chemicals rule the brain. People are robots.

But who will be interested in my theories? No one. (Except He who originated them.) He lost interest in me and that's offensive, so I left. First he went home, where, when one must return, they have to take you in (Covington, KY). Then I talked him into coming back and we went on to St. Petersburg in Florida.

In St. Petersburg, the palmetto bugs flavored everything. I still think of those crisp greasy brown wings whenever I picture the town. The bugs were dirty amber cockroaches, but two inches long, capable of flight, and not afraid of daylight. We bought a blender at a garage sale and went on a binge of frothy tropical drinks and left it wet and the bugs would converge on it.

He had no patience for me.

I'm not going to be a baby and whine about things as they are. It's hard though. I don't know too much about sobriety. There'll be plenty of time for that when I'm dead.

He was changing. When I look back at it now I can understand it better. He used heroin for a while in Memphis too. That might have contributed to his unhappiness and impatience. But I'm afraid he was outgrowing me, "growing away," rather. It has no meaning, it's just life, it's just "things." It was torture at the time, but isn't everything? Life is like blinding sunlight and even when it's good it's too much (too little? of too). That's why drugs are necessary.

"Payne Whitney" is such a pretty name for a hospital. The Paynes and the Whitneys would only put their names on the best places, wouldn't they? (Like in *The Shining* when Barry Nelson is showing Jack and Wendy around and tells them that the "best people" stayed at the Overlook . . .) I much prefer it to "Bellevue." "Bellevue" has a sweeter sound, but it's a rough place. "Payne Whitney" might sound like razor blades but it's in order to suggest a pretty machine for making you feel better. It would be terrible if I didn't have the clinic to come to when I need it.

I have kind of a crush on the meek boy in the room next door. (Why can I not think of anyone I like without thinking of their sexual areas??? It's always been my weakness . . . I do try not to "take advantage" of people though.) I also have a crush on his sister who's been a patient here too! It gives me such pleasure to look at him and find not only himself but his sweet sister in that face. Then again sometimes it scares me a little. I asked him once if he was really his sister and it wasn't a very good opening line.

Right now it's that kind of morning where outside's been manifesting mild vapor all night, like mist from an atomizer, and the sky, the color of marble, the color of animal fat, yields a light that's a not unpleasant sick yellow. Things seem soft and eternal and slightly artificial. It's as if everything is quietly commiserating with me. I know it must smell good outside. I wish I could open the hospital window.

They hand out a sheet of "stress management" proverbs to all the patients, recommending we repeat them to ourselves when we're relaxed so that they'll pop into our heads when we're stressed and we can use them then. In other words: *all the time.* Do I really want Anonymous in my head going, "He who is content with little has everything," every waking hour? It could be worse I guess. There could be someone in my head going, "Your dick is turning to spinach." The sayings mostly boil down, like spinach, to: "Lower your expectations." It's kind of Buddhist really. I actually like spinach. First noble truth: Life is suffering. Second noble truth: The suffering is a result of desire. (Third noble truth: Get over it.) The one from Abe Lincoln is good: "People are about as happy as they make up their minds to be." (Or, as Bodhidharma put it, "The external world is only a manifestation of the activities of the mind.") They know we're hopeless so they just want us to know it's fine to be hopeless.

20

California and Florida are like the butt and dick of America. California, like Jennifer Lopez, gets all of the attention, doubtless because it's so fat and broad and also because Hollywood is there, bright sink of egress. But Florida dangles tawdry and tangy too, home to major theme amusement parks. America is a big pretty she-male and Paul and T. had chosen to abide in its stunted penis.

It was too hot there. There was too much sun and smell and grit, and the air-conditioning was almost as oppressive. Incontinence was rampant.

I woke up just before dawn thinking about someone I know who's not doing well. I almost cried but not quite.

Thick heavy ribbons from the sky of slow golden syrup form a sideways stack of slanting 8's that slump at once.

One day Paul came back to the house in his thriftstore tropical shirt swinging his pink mesh bag of plastic-wrapped smoked mullet and T. started laughing at him while he was coming up the sidewalk.

Paul threw the fish at him and screamed. Despite everything, with nowhere to go, his innocence was too offended. He unwrapped the fish and threw them at T. again. He stumbled through the house, snatching possessions and what money there was, and turned and fled to the bus station. He bought a ticket back to Memphis. He called his mother. (His wife wouldn't talk to him anymore.) T. arrived at the bus station just as Paul was boarding. As T. swore remorse and promised love and kindness, making every argument to keep Paul there, at the same time he was inevitably mocking him for having no better idea of what to do with himself than go back to that Tennessee city that he hated.

On the way to Memphis Paul sniffed the fish on his fingers. He couldn't call T. because they had no phone in Florida. He wrote to him, gloating in defiance, "Did you think you could abuse me forever?" and he mailed the letter at the first rest stop. Seated again in the coursing bus, frowning mournfully, his bulging right temple pressed against the big cold plate glass, he felt like a silly queen, like someone who'd be called "Miss," facial stubble and balding dome notwithstanding. He felt like an older woman. He knew it would annoy T. but he couldn't help himself. It was like his butt was flabby and his makeup was smeared and his eyes were red. Like his tits were little floppy tubes and his young boyfriend just laughed at him. This was not Paul! He wrote T. another letter, a more manly independent letter, he thought, saying nothing was left for himself, that perhaps it was time for drastic action. He would kill himself! If only he had some drugs. He felt like his insides were aligned in wide vertical stripes.

His mother might actually be coming to Memphis. She'd said she was going to.

All right, so I am a poet and not a good father, not a temperate person. I like to be drunk. My god, a dry martini! Really! I want things to happen at times ("*At times*": It's a phrase of his that I absorbed!), and if that's weakness I am weak, and then I may not know how to make the things happen that I want to happen and I flail, I get confused. And if I'm drunk and flailing at the same time I may do something stupid. The Church has helped me as it helps all (like a good mother), but I hadn't found the Church at that time, and I made a mistake but it really hurt me more than anyone else.

The worst thing was when I could hear him talking to me as if I was a fool. But I am a fool! So don't talk to me that way. So he wasn't a fool. He needed me to be whole himself.

So Brown Felix peddles me that little thirty-two. I'd never even shot a pistol. I was so drunk. I wasn't sober that whole week. I remember thinking the gun looked like a black Florida, with it's little silver Smith and Wesson medallion right about at St. Petersburg too. The thing was a joke, some play on animal nature, like fake vomit or a fart cushion. It was so blunt and thickly forged that, despite its small size, it seemed more like a garden tool than a purveyor of death. I fired it once in the motel room, at the ceiling across the room. It did make a person feel powerful to have an effect at a distance by pointing like that. It felt great in the hand.

And then there was my mother who came south when I told her I was going to kill myself if Carol wouldn't take me back, and when T. called the room my mother told him I was going to enlist in the army! I really was thinking that. And he came to Memphis too, and when he saw what I was like, and took money from me again, and my mother was screaming at me, and T. was leaving forever, I didn't know what to do! I winged him with that little gun. The freedom of youth! He was hardly hurt at all.

The freedom of youth: I had freedom to make mistakes of

judgement, emotional mistakes; he had freedom to be interested in things. I have learned some things from my mistakes, and who knows what became of him? I think he lost interest. I think the things that interested him were reduced in number, greatly reduced. So who came out best in the long run?

I was in jail for eighteen months for what I did. He went off never to be seen again, for all practical purposes. I don't want to talk about it. It's time for my medication. I'm glad I don't have to take those drugs that make your eyes too bright anymore.

***

But, to contradict ourselves, it is enough just to name things, if you know their names. I don't! Maybe that means my whole life is wasted. I'm melodramatic. But it would be nice to have that kind of suicide: one of recognition that one'd forgotten what life was for. At least it would mean you'd noticed. You'd go out on a good note. The most beautiful poets detail the names of things I just realized again for this moment, but purely defined, all words are names, obviously: to repeat it is no achievement . . .

> What would I like to give you?
> Beads, a steel rose, a book?
> No, flowers, roses, real roses
> —Maréchal Niel, Gloire de
> Dijon, Variegata di Bologna,
> Madame Alfred Carrière, Souvenir
> de la Malmaison, Georg Arends,
> Prince Camille de Rohan: or,
> Maybe better, homelier,

Canadian columbine, rusty red
(Or rather orange?), spurred,
Hanging down, drying, turning
Brown, turning up, a cup
Full of fine black seeds
That sparkle, wake-robin,
Trillium, a dish of rich
Soft moss stuck with little
Flowers from the woods—
Bloodroot, perhaps

Ha ha! But it's not true! The classic names (of flora here) alone are kind of dull when you pluck them from their poem (no, they're not), which poem ("A Name Day") relates other names of many descriptions (names of all descriptions!) too, in other lines, for instance: Anne, the mother of the Virgin, her name detailed as a Latinization of the Hebrew name Hannah. "Mary, sustain us in our need," he prays a moment later. The poet's eighty-six-year-old mother having a frightening spasm, unwilling to go to the doctor, alone with her somewhat helpless poet son: the true names of fear and pity and love, which are anecdotes and images, as are the names of flowers, flowers word-imagined into being as gifts for the poet's friend's Name Day in another country. And truthfully the words are as effective for the music of their arrangement as much as anything: "rusty red (Or rather orange?), spurred, Hanging down, drying, turning Brown, turning up, a cup" (prickly red descending into brown that twists upward at its edges as a cup— one remove and it's a kind of sodomy!) and "Trillium, a dish of rich Soft moss stuck with little Flowers from the woods—Bloodroot, perhaps [...]" It's naming things musically, with the intellectual content of the succession-of-words' implications being like the hooks and ropes that prevent one from falling into the abyss, or like the incidental nourishment value of a beautiful and beautifully presented plate of supernaturally good-tasting haute cuisine.

Of course no writing can rival reality, but reality's easy. Just exist and there it is. I remember him trying to tell me the way a sweeping landscape near the Hudson made him feel. How he was absorbed or obliterated by it, and how happy it made him because it seemed like such a perfect resolution, like the final piece of a puzzle. It took him in and its color was not changed, nothing was ruffled, there was no sign of him at all. And then he said, "But of course, that's not really what happens. Not at all. It's just a mildly effective thing to say about it." Still, a person has to make a living somehow.

21

Yesterday Joe Storch told me he thought he'd seen Randall's mother in front of the hospital a few days ago with someone else who he thought looked like she could be her daughter. He told me that yesterday afternoon. Strange as it might seem, I didn't really think much about it. He'd only met T.'s mother once, thirty years ago, and he'd never met T.'s sister. The mother always had a distinctive appearance though. She wore dark dresses that looked like they came from the 19th century: long and heavy and multilayered. Joe said the other woman was exactly the same but a daughter's age. And what's the big deal? I know how to find that old lady if I want, even though I haven't talked to her in forever–she started hanging up on me years ago, telling me poor Terence had died. And, sure, something or other could always bring her to New York. Joe mentioned her like he was just talking about all the ghosts everywhere himself . . . But when he left, I started thinking. (What else do I have to do here???) What if it really was his crazy old peasant mother and sister?

So I asked the nurse I love if she'd check for me and see if there was anyone by his name in the hospital. She came back and told me "yes." That is what I said. It's him. T. is alive and here in this hospital right now!!! What is going on?

He was dead. That's what we were told. I thought he was dead. We all did. His mother said so. Nobody ever heard anything about him.

I don't know what to do.

I couldn't just go surprise him anyway. Oh my god.

This is too weird.

The nurse said he has some jungle disease, tropical disease, that he'd come from South America for treatment.

He used to talk about the Amazon sometimes.

I'll write a note to him.

What the fuck?!?!

What could have become of him? What could he be like now? I wonder if he's a scholar? But then why would he be in South America? On the other hand, South America sounds exactly like him, with how disgusted civilization made him and how much he liked the woods. But is it possible with all his intelligence and his abilities that he could have failed to make an impression in the world? Of course. Worldly things are stupid. Doubtless all the most interesting people are completely unknown. And anyway he's famous in a way.

Maybe I could take care of him. How old will he be? Forty-two. Imagine, forty-two.

I only saw him once more, for one afternoon, a little while after I got out of jail. In 1975. He was twenty-one: the only time I've ever seen him as "an adult." He was living in New Orleans. He did seem really hard bitten. Not bitter, but just tough and held-in. He told me to give him any money I had. I was a little drunk. He pushed me out of his door and closed it and when I didn't go away he opened the door and pushed me hard. He was penniless, as always, but there were books and notebooks in his room. He said he wasn't writing though. It was like he'd forgotten about it, as if it was a childish hobby, like building plastic models. He had books on architecture and engineering and geography and he appeared to be studying them. Not that that means anything. He was always studying something.

It's true he told me once that he thought Lévi-Strauss's *Tristes Tropiques* was the great book of the 20th century, greater than any novel. But then he also said that about a book on meteorology he found that was basically nothing but clouds.

Oh my god, I wonder how ill he is? I don't want to tell anybody about this. I've got to see him first. I wonder if he knows his poems are published and he's famous.

I can get permission for an hour pass, I'm sure. Oh man, I've got to work this out in my head.

What can I write him? "Mr. T.! Sir!" Ha ha.

Dear Randall T.,

I've just discovered: 1) that you're alive, and 2) that you're in this hospital! I'm here too. (I'm in the psych ward as I usually am for two or three weeks a year, but nothing's really wrong with me.) Obviously if you'd positively wished to have any contact with me all these years you could have, but I hope you will read this note with a little charity.

It's hard not to write you a love note! I've been think-ing about you so much lately. Your name has been spoken a lot as you may not know. Did you know that all of us thought you were dead? But you probably didn't care to think about us.

Will you let me visit you? I only want to see your face and hear your voice. I ask nothing of you I swear. It's all I ask to see your face and hear your voice—I will be able to extract everything from that. I promise I expect nothing more and will not ask for anything else. May I visit you?

Love and respect,

Paul (Vaughn)

Oh God it's awful, but I don't know what to do.

***

I'm too old for this. He is dead. He died here. He died today. He'd been in the hospital almost a week, but he died today. Or yesterday, the same day I discovered he was here. I found out late yesterday afternoon when I tried to get to him. I've been up all night. It's 10:00 A.M. I've just seen him.

Early this morning I had an appointment about my operation and my nurse friend got the assignment to escort me and on the way she snuck me down to the sub-basement where they keep the bodies.

I found his body in the morgue. His skin was very dark and creased. I never would have recognized him. I kept saying to myself that I thought he was dead already anyway. But I knew him so well for a little while. Somehow it felt like that was being torn away. Because as I stared at his face I could of course find the face of the boy in it. The corpse, eyes closed, looked very brave. That's all I could see. I could still see his bravery in it. But it didn't have a personality. It just penetrated like an arrow pointing at everything that's gone. He was brave and so was the corpse, like a statue heroically, pathetically attempting to represent something beyond its means. It wasn't him, because He was alive. Thank God it looked asleep. It was like a sign pointing at everything I myself can't reach, that I don't understand. I can't stand it. How can anything be believed? I closed my eyes. But that was worse. I turned away. The corpse was horrible. It made everything alive seem ridiculously innocent, but I turned away. He looked at emotions as a scientist, but there are things I know more about than he did. I know that love is real.

RICHARD HELL is a novelist, poet, essayist, and diarist who first came to public attention in the mid-seventies as a musician and songwriter. His album *Blank Generation* was seminal to "punk." His books include the novel *Go Now*; *Hot and Cold*, a collection of poems, essays, lyrics, notebooks, and pictures; and *Artifact: Notebooks from Hell 1974–1980*. He grew up in Lexington, Kentucky, but has lived in New York since he was seventeen. He's at work now on a book of memories.

In addition to the trade paperback, this book
is published in a cloth edition limited to forty copies.
Twenty-six are lettered A–Z and signed by the author;
fourteen, *hors commerce*, are numbered 1–14 and
signed by the author.